WHAT I THOUGHT I WANTED

A NOVEL

By E'nise

What I thought I wanted

A Second Time Media & Communications Book/published by arrangement with the author.

Printing History
First printing: May 2009
Copyright 2007 by E'nise
Cover design and production by Brenda Lewis www.ubangi-design.com

For bulk order information address:
Second Time Media & Communications LLC,
P.O. Box 401367
Redford, MI 48240-1367

ISBN: 978-0-9815162-1-9

Printed in the United States of America

Dedication

*This novel is dedicated to my Mother & Grandmother.
Without you two, there would be no me. While my
Father was not around and did not have time for me,
you two raised me with all the love and affection
I needed. I thank you for loving me and teaching me
how to love others.
You always told me I could do anything if I set my
mind to it.
Look at me now, I did it!*

E'nise

Acknowledgements

First and foremost, thank you God for giving me the ability to be creative and write. For blessing me with the gift of life and love within my life. I thank you for each day you give me with my family and loved ones.

To my Hubby, you are the best. With all the trials and tribulations we've been through, God continues to bless us. We have definitely proved we are the "strong" and we will "survive." Thanks for being here with me to see this project through. I love you.

I would like to first say, "I love you, son" to my nephew. Although I did not have you, I couldn't love you anymore than if you were my own child. We have been through a lot together and we have a lot more to go through in this life. I will always be here for you, just like a Mother would. No matter how old you get, you will always be my baby.

To My Grandma, you have been my "road dog" all my life, from Kindergarten to today. As far back as I can remember, it was me and you. Thank you for all the pep talks about men, relationships, and for allowing me to be able to tell you anything without you judging me. I love you unconditionally and you know I would do anything for you.

To My Mother, "my pillar of strength." You have always been the strongest woman I know. Despite your unhappy beginnings, the pain you went through carrying me, and the bad relationships *we* made it through together, I always remember you being strong. You make me be the warrior I am today. Even when I fall, I think of you. I get up and dust myself off to fight another day. This is so emotional just putting these words together. You've always been a hard worker and provider for the family. If I never told you or didn't tell you enough, I appreciate all your sacrifices, work and effort into raising me and Trina. I know it wasn't a picnic, but you sure made it seem like one. Thanks Ma, I love ya!

Thank you to Gina-Boo who finally gave me the kick in the butt to write. I guess I was a lot like you, I can't believe I did it.

Thanks Betty for giving me the "man up" speeches when I felt like giving up. Although you may not have understood all aspects of what I was doing with this thing, you did your best to keep me on track. Thanks.

Jackie, thank you for being my first reader. I'll never forget the night you called me and told me how good it was and to "Hurry up and finish it!" You've always been good to me and given me the greatest advice. Don't ever change. Keep being that sassy lady who shoots straight from the hip!

To my brother Jody, now I've finished my first novel, I'm looking for your book to be coming soon. We made a deal, and a deal is a deal. Love ya, Bro.

To my Uncle Marvin Hill, thanks for coming into my Mother's life and providing so much love and joy. She is so proud to say, "My Brother" and I am so proud to say, "My Uncle." While it's only been a short time since we have became close, we have a lifetime to grow even closer.

To my cousin Kim and Aunt Ruby, you two are the best family a girl could have. Thanks for always being supportive and loving me as much as I love you.

I almost forgot the one person who has listened to me over ten years. No matter what I have ever called you about, you have always been there for me to listen. Whether it was a disappointing relationship, a bad day at work, or such much on me, I thought I couldn't go any further, you have always been a friend to me. You and I are a lot alike in ways, we should have been related. I'll always be your best friend and you mine. Thanks for the encouragement in every aspect of my life, including this book. Stan, thank you for being the very best friend a girl could have.

My girl, a.k.a, Unforgettable. You've grown a lot over the years. You will and still are like a sister to me. I love you.

I would also like to take this time to acknowledge Erica N. Martin. I true "Sista". Thank you for welcoming me into the Second Time Media family with open arms. For giving me honesty and sincerity every step of the way, I appreciate you. You told me I would get more excited as time went on, and you were right. I can't believe I'm writing acknowledgements for *my* book. You are truly gifted in this industry. Your attitude and experience in this industry will take you just where you want to go. Thank you so much. I cannot just call you "my Publisher" anymore, you are truly my FRIEND.

To the rest of my friends, family and loved ones, I say "thank you" for being apart of my life. I may have not mentioned everyone by name, but it doesn't mean you don't hold importance in my life and especially in my heart. My journey has just begun, ride with me till the end.

E'nise.

E'nise

What I thought I wanted

Prologue

September 3, 2006

"What's that noise? *Beep, beep, beep.* Man, I can't open my eyes. *Beep, beep, beep.* It's so hard to try and open my eyes. *Beep, beep, beep.* Damn! I can't move anything. Finally, I began to force my eyes open, but everything looks real hazy. As I struggle to focus, that beeping sound is getting faster."

Just as I finally begin to focus, a nurse appears.

"Oh my, you've opened your eyes!"

She left the room, and I heard her calling for a doctor.

"Oh my God, how did I get here? I can't remember…how did I get here? I got all these machines hooked up to me and I can't seem to move my legs or arms. I wonder how long I've been here.

Just as I was struggling to remember, the nurse reappears with the doctor.

"Well…well…well, I'm Dr. Lyson. I'm your regular attending physician. You've been through quite an ordeal."

As he was talking to me, he began to check my pupils with one of those pin lights. Checking my chart and then he began to ask me questions.

"Do you know how long you've been here?"

I slowly turned my head from left to right.

He then began to do something by my bedside.

"Can you feel this?"

Again, I turned my head from left to right to indicate no. I was wondering what he was doing.

He spoke to me again, "What about this?"

Again I indicated no, realizing I couldn't speak. No matter how badly I wanted to verbally answer all of his questions, I just couldn't speak.

He then moved to the end of the bed and I could see him touch my toes on my left foot, but before he could even ask, I was wondering why I couldn't feel it. I struggled hard to feel his touch. I wanted to feel his touch. I began to get upset, and the more upset I got, the faster the beeps got again. Tears began to form in my eyes.

He quickly came back to my bedside, "Calm down, try not to get upset. This situation may be only temporary. We will need to run some additional tests. You've been through a lot and it will take time to rehabilitate. Can you understand what I am saying to you?"

I nodded slowly up and down to indicate yes. I began to try and open my mouth to talk. My mouth was moving, but no words were coming out.

Dr. Lyson began to explain to me, "You've been here for over a month, and I'm sure your family and friends will be anxious to know you have finally awakened. You have had a constant stream of support. Not a day goes by without someone coming to check your status. You are very lucky to have survived your ordeal. You are a very strong woman."

As the doctor smiled slightly he said, "Your family and friends said you are a fighter. You've had three major surgeries since you were brought in through emergency with all three being very successful. Now I need you to bear with me while I check the rest of your extremities for paralysis. Remember to stay calm, and tell me if you can feel my touches."

He moved to the other side of the bed and spoke to the nurse who was standing by jotting down information onto my chart.

"Please go and contact her family and friends listed on her chart."

She left the room with my chart in her hand. He touched my hand and at the same time asked if I could feel it. To my surprise, I did. I nodded to indicate that I could. I was so happy to be able to feel something. He then moved back down to the end of my bed and touched my other foot, but I couldn't feel that. He told me he was going to apply a little pressure, but I still didn't feel anything. Even though I couldn't feel either of my feet or my other hand, I was happy to be alive.

I was so preoccupied with the test the doctor was performing on me that I didn't give much thought to the pain my body was enduring. As he began to note my chart, I looked at all the different machines working to keep me alive.

I tried hard to remember what had happened to me. It's funny, I could understand everything the Doctor was saying to me, but I couldn't remember how I ended up in the hospital.

After he finished writing notes in my chart and speaking into a small tape recorder, he appeared back at my bedside. He asked me a series of questions.

"Do you know what hospital you are in?"

I gestured to him that I didn't.

"Do you know what month this is?"

Again I shook my head, *'no'*.

"What year this is?"

Again no.

The doctor began to look more serious, maybe even more concerned. As he leaned in even closer, he looked directly into my eyes and posed the most profound question yet, "Do you know who you are?"

With a feeling of doom, I looked at Dr. Lyson with tears in my eyes, and slowly turned my head from left to right telling him no.

He told me that was all for now and walked away speaking into his recorder, but the only thing that kept going through my head was..."Who am I?"

Chapter 1
June 10, 2005

It's my birthday and my girls are picking me up in a minute. Out of the 365 days in a year, this is the one day that I have to be cute! Got my booty shorts on with a red Gucci halter top, guaranteed to make heads turn! Just as I was fixing my hair, my phone rang. I looked over at the caller ID and answered it.

"What up, Stacy?"

"Nothing girl, I just picked up Lisa and Kim. We are on our way."

"Yeah! Well, hurry up."

Stacy managed to tell me through her laugh, "Shut up bitch, and *don't get bossy!*"

We laughed and hung up. My girls are cool. We've been friends ever since orientation at General Motors. We all got hired on the same day. I guess you can say we're like family. We've been best friends for over five years now.

My girl Stacy is wild as hell. She's the girl most fellas want. Thick, chocolate skin and an ass that makes guys do a double take. Not to mention, it's accentuated by her small ass waist. Stacy is all about her paper. My girl works plenty of O.T., and will still trick with some of the guys in the plant and outside of the plant for that matter, for no less than an extra $500.00 in her pocket.

My girl loves to shop and Somerset Mall (the high priced mall) in Troy, Michigan is the only place she shops. Neiman Marcus and Saks Fifth Avenue are among her favorite stores.

With all that money she makes plus driving a drop top Benz CLK 350, you would think her crib would rival those on MTV's Cribs. Wrong! She still stays with her mom over in the University District. Don't get me wrong, the houses over there are the bomb. A beautiful upscale community in Detroit, but the other girls and I are always trying to get Ms. Stacy to strike out on her own. Stacy always says she and her mother are like best friends rather than mother and daughter. They hang and drink together, so why should she move?

My girl Lisa is what most guys call, 'straight hood'. She lives on the Eastside of Detroit, off of Mack & Bewick. Believe me, it's not cool. We're always trying to get her to move to a better neighborhood, but she won't budge.

The house she lives in was her mother's. She died from cancer a few years ago and left Lisa and her four year old daughter, Simone, the house.

Now Lisa is a very pretty girl; tall, slender with legs for days. She kind of reminds you of a thinner Laila Ali. She should have been a model. Most people think she's gay or bisexual because of the way she talks and carries herself. She doesn't get off into all the skirts and trendy clothes. Lisa is comfortable in a pair of baggy jeans, gym shoes and oversized shirts.

She is tough and ain't taking no shit, unless your name is Ronald Sims. Ron is her freeloading ass baby daddy who pops in and out of her and Simone's life. He stays with her occasionally without dropping down a dime to pay a damn thing. He's one of those men that can't pay the cost, but wants to be the boss.

Now don't get me wrong, Ron is fine, but he don't do nothing but smoke weed and drink. He stays on medical more than he works. Lisa met him at a cabaret we went to and the rest was history. I regret taking her shopping and helping her look like a runway model that night. Shit, if it wasn't for my insistence, Ron wouldn't be such a thorn in her side. Of course then, we wouldn't have Simone…we all love Simone and she loves all her Aunties. So I guess, at least one good thing came out of their relationship.

Then there's Kim. Kim is the "conscience" of the group as well as the oldest in our crew. She's always trying to keep us from making the same mistakes she claims she has made. Now to me, Kim has it going on. A nice crib in Southfield's Lathrup

Village, she's going to school for Nursing and is determined to not be at the plant for thirty years.

Kim is a short sister with a short hairdo she keeps in tact. No bad hair days for this sister. She has flair like a lawyer and carries herself like a woman on a mission. Almond colored skin and a little on the plus side, she dresses for success outside of the walls of General Motors.

She is originally from Chicago and moved to Michigan two years before getting hired at GM. Men are always trying to get at Kim, but she turns all of them away. She says she's been through enough with men and will not let them slow her down in achieving her goals.

She's got one son, Malcolm. He's fourteen years old and an honor roll student. She had him when she was eighteen. Malcolm is her pride and joy. The funny thing about Kim is that besides not dating, she never talks about Malcolm's dad or her past. It's almost like her life started seven years ago in Michigan. Go figure.

Well enough about them hoes…back to me. I mean it is my birthday. My name is Amber Smith and today, I am twenty-seven years old. I don't have any kids, so I'm baby daddy drama free. Working at General Motors keeps money in the bank, with a black on black H3 Hummer in my driveway. I own a gorgeous condo in a small community called Harbortown located in downtown Detroit.

I'm short and thick dark skinned brick house. Most would say I'm shaped like a Coca Cola bottle. The old men at the plant glorify me as a pretty black girl. But what the hell is that supposed to mean? Just because I'm dark skinned, I can't be cute? Just like the statement some fools make, "She dark skin, but she cute." Anyways, my cocoa brown skin is flawless. Oh yeah! I am a dime piece!

I'm tired of dating stupid ass men with no job, looking for someone to take care of them. I'm at a point in my life where

I want to settle down and have a family. I'm hoping a real man finds me. Like the bible says, "Whosoever finds a wife, findeth a good thing." So, I'm still dating and waiting for the man I will be a good 'thing' for. But for right now its ladies night, and my girl Stacy just came through the gatehouse blowing the horn outside my condo, so I'm out the door. Oh yeah, it's my birthday…it's my birthday!

Chapter 2

AMBER

"Girl, I ain't ate this much in a long time, but a free birthday meal from my girls at Fishbones can make a sister eat. Where we headed to next ladies?"

Stacy put her margarita down and said, "Let's head up on Jefferson to the liquor store, get some drinks and hit Belle Isle."

The sun was just going down when we hit the strip. Four beautiful ladies in that red hot, drop top Benz. All eyes were on us.

Stacy was bumpin the music and we were all singing and feeling good. We pulled into a parking spot on the strip, cracked open the liquor and started making our signature drink of Grey Goose, Grape pucker, 7-Up, with a splash of Patron. We called it 'Purple Passion'.

Lisa fired up a blunt as Stacy cranked up the radio. Just then an old jam came on.

Kim started singing first, *"Just got paid, its Friday Night, party hunting…"*

That was the cue for the rest of us to join in. We started singing and dancing to the song. It only took a minute for one of us to mess up and we all started laughing.

Belle Isle was jumpin! You see all kinds of rides rolling through here. From old school to the most expensive foreign rides. Everybody wants to be seen.

We were feeling real good, until Lisa's phone rang. We gave each other that look as Lisa walked away from us and answered it. Next thing you know, she was arguing.

I asked Stacy, "Who she talking to?"

Stacy smacked her lips and responded, "Probably her lazy ass baby daddy. You know he always seems to smell when she having fun."

Ron hates to see Lisa get out the house and have a good time. Just like most no good men, he don't want to step up and be the provider in her life, but can't stand the thought of someone else getting his good thing.

Stacy was getting mad watching Lisa get upset on the phone and spoke louder, "That's why I don't fuck with no man for free. Shit like that…wasting time arguing with a dude who ain't giving you nothing but a headache."

We paused for a second when we heard Lisa say,

"Just stay the fuck away from me and Simone. I'm tired of you and your shit. You don't want to do nothing, don't want to work or spend any time with your daughter. The only time I see you're sorry ass is when your medical check is gone. Then you wanna come to my house at 3 in the morning whispering that 'I love you' bullshit. That ain't working no more brotha, sorry."

I went over to her and said, "Hang up that damn phone. Fuck that dead beat Dad. It's my birthday and we having a good time."

Kim looked at me with that motherly look and said,

"Girl, leave Lisa alone. She'll know when she's done."

Turning away from Kim, I saw about ten motorcycles coming our way. Damn, I love to see guys on bikes. The bigger the bike, the more I like it. They pulled over on the strip next to us. That was the first time I saw Ameri. He was riding a black and silver Hyabusi. I couldn't take my eyes off of him. When he took his helmet off, our eyes met. He was so fine!

We must have stared at each other for what seemed like a lifetime. He looked about 6'3"and had to be at least 210 lbs. He had chestnut brown skin, a light mustache and goatee with full lips and the warmest eyes that went right through me. He finally smiled and I smiled back.

He started talking to his boys when Stacy hit me to wake me out of my slumber saying, "Damn bitch! Put your tongue back in your mouth!"

15

"Shut up, Stacy," I said halfheartedly. "I was just admiring God's creation and applauding him for his work."

Lisa finally got off the phone with Ron. Her bubbly attitude had turned sour. No smiles, no laughter. I hated Ron for stealing my girl's joy. I tried to cheer her up.

"Come on Lisa, have a drink and hit this blunt. Girl, look at them fine ass motorcycle riders over there."

Lisa smiled a little, "Yeah, they are fine."

Stacy hit the blunt and told Lisa, "Girl, you already know Ron ain't right."

Her smile quickly vanished, "Yeah, I know, but I just wish he would get it together. Not for just me, but for his daughter. With him working at Chrysler and me at General Motors, we could have a good life."

Stacy looked at Lisa with that 'Are you serious look'.

"Look Lisa, Ron is who he is. Now you are off the phone with him and we got purple passion and some 'get high' waiting on you, so what you gonna do? Bring everybody down with you?"

Lisa stared at Stacy for a moment, and let out a big sigh, "You're right. Let's celebrate our girl's birthday!"

We all yelled, and toasted, and in unison, hit our cups together stating, "Friends to the end!"

As we laughed, I felt a hand touch my shoulder from behind. My girls looked like they saw Jason or Freddy behind me! My heart felt like it dropped in my shoe. I turned around and looked into the eyes of a man I knew I had to have.

He introduced himself, "Hi, my name is Ameri. I've been watching you for a little while and decided to take my chances in meeting you. May I ask, what your name is?"

I almost couldn't get it out, but with the help of Stacy bumping me, I finally spoke and introduced myself.

"I'm Amber, nice to meet you."

"Nice to meet you Amber."

His dimples were deep and amazing. He was a real gentleman. Sexy seemed to ooze out of him. He smelled sooo good. I wondered what kind of cologne he had on. Whatever it was, it was just right with his body chemistry.

I turned around to see where my girls were. Stacy was talking to some guy parked on the strip in a brand new Suburban with spinners. Kim and Lisa were sitting on Stacy's car, probably talking about Ron's trifling ass.

Ameri again captured my attention.

"Looks like your girls are alright. Now can I have an opportunity to get to know you better? I mean it must have been meant for me to meet you, I almost stayed home tonight."

We talked for over an hour. Talking with him felt unusually comfortable for meeting someone less than two hours ago.

Turns out Ameri lives in Westland, works for the G.M. plant in Romulus, and has two sons. One is six years old and the other is three. He was with the kids' mother up until a few months ago. He said it would take more than an hour to explain his complicated situation with the kids' mom.

We exchanged numbers with the commitment to go out real soon. That night my girls and I piled back into Stacy's car and headed off the park. Lisa asked me if I enjoyed my birthday. My mind reflected on Ameri, with the scent of his cologne still in my nostrils. I replied,

"I sure did…I sure did."

Chapter 3
<u>AMBER</u>

I was at work when I felt the vibration of my cell phone on my hip. Once I removed it from my side and checked the caller ID, I quickly moved off my job to a quiet spot and answered.

"Hello."

On the other end, I heard his voice, "Hey beautiful, how are you?"

I replied with a grin I'm sure he could detect over the phone, "Fine."

"Good. I was wondering if we could meet after work for a drink?"

With excitement I quickly said, "Sure. Where do you want to meet?"

He thought for a moment, "What about Applebee's (Ford Road in Dearborn?"

I wasn't feeling that, I know that was convenient f but that was too far for me. I told him we would have to somewhere near a major expressway to make it conver both of us. We finally came to the agreement to meet Friday's at Fairlane Mall. That works for me coming downtown and him coming from Canton. We agree(p.m. I hung up the phone with a permanent smile p my face.

It was break time now, so I walked over to {

As I walked up, she was talking to Mitch. M worked at the plant for more than thirty years. Besi job, he has an illegal hustle on the side. He's the nu and loan shark in the plant. You could play your lo and borrow money in one stop with him.

Although Mitch has a wife at home, Stacy l messing around with him for years.

18

"Hey Mitch. What's up Stacy?"

Mitch spoke and looked back at Stacy as he began to walk away. Stacy frowned a little.

"What's wrong with you Stacy?" I asked.

"Girl, Mitch's ass wants me to come to his house…his wife is spending a week in Florida with their daughter, she just had a baby. His freaky old ass loves for me to come over there and have sex with him."

I immediately became afraid for her. I mean, what if his wife comes home? Or if the neighbors tell his wife about the young girl they see coming over, thinking maybe Stacy is their daughter.

I couldn't help but to speak up and say something to her.

"Damn! Stacy don't you get scared going to that woman's house?"

In her usually sassy attitude she said, "Look Amber, it's not like she knows and as long as Mitch is given up them dollars, I'm given up this ass."

After standing there looking at my friend, I replied,

"Well, that's not what I came over here for. Ameri called me. We are meeting for drinks at Friday's."

"That's cool girl." She said smiling.

"Yeah, I'm excited. I haven't felt this excited in a while. Well girl, it's almost time for me to get back to my job, see you later."

She chimed in right behind me, "Ok, girl see you later."

As I turned to walk away, I turned around towards my friend again, "Stacy, be careful."

She looked at me, knowing all I have for her is love and

"I will…you be careful too."

LISA

I know I had two hundred dollars in this drawer.

"Mom, can I have a popsicle? I turned away momentarily from looking through my drawers again, and for the third time told my daughter, "Wait Simone, mommy is looking for something. Go back and watch T.V. As soon as I'm finished, I will give you a popsicle, ok?"

"Ok Mom," said Simone with an understanding nod.

I closed the last drawer on my dresser and immediately went to my cell phone.

"Hello…Ron, tell me you didn't take my money!"

He struggled to answer my question,

"Oh hey baby! Now, baby you know I love you."

"I don't want to hear that shit, Ron. Did you take my money?"

He tried to explain, "Well baby, I needed some money for my prescriptions and my doctor's visit. You know Blue Cross don't pay for my office visits. I'm gonna put it back as soon as I go back to work. I should be going back to work …"

Before he could finish his explanation, I hung up the phone, sat on the side of my bed and cried. This is something I've done so many times before; cry and cry about something Ron has done to affect me and my daughter's life, and constantly question why I don't just let him go.

I've never told my friends the complete truth about Ron. He's been stealing from me for years. Drained my savings account by stealing my ATM card, and even stole what few pieces of jewelry I had. Luckily he never got to the ring my Mother left me. Only reason he probably didn't get that is because I wear it everyday.

I finally had to change the locks on my house because he would take the televisions, stereos, or whatever else he could sell for a quick buck. Ron acted like he was on drugs at times, but I always looked the other way.

Because of my neighborhood, he would always say someone must have broken in. I called the police once when the next alleged break-in occurred, only to have them look at me as if I was stupid.

I explained that someone broke in. The officers' searched the whole house then came back to where I was waiting.

One of the officers looked at me and said, "Uh, ma'am, there were no signs of forced entry. No windows were broken. Does anyone else have a key to your house?"

My heart fell as I replied, "Yes, my boyfriend."

The officer looked at me sternly, "Well Ma'am, I suggest you start with him."

That was the last time I called the police. It took a few more 'break-ins' before I changed the locks and only allowed Ron over when I was home.

I had to get an alarm system, because one time he broke in and was in the house when I came home. Man, if the rest of the girls knew what I had been going through, they would have cussed me out and called me stupid. They just don't know how many times I've called myself stupid.

As I dried my eyes and got up from the side of the bed, I walked into the living room where Simone was. She'd fallen asleep waiting for her popsicle.

I stood there looking at my daughter thinking about how much I love her. I felt bad for all I'm putting her through with her dad. As a little girl, I always wanted to have kids and give them a household with a mom and dad, but never did I imagine raising a family under these circumstances.

When Ron was sober and working, he treated Simone and I like his queen and princess. The problem was that there weren't too many memories like that.

What I thought I Wanted

I picked my daughter up from the floor and carried her into her room. Laying her in the bed, I gently placed a kiss on my little angel's forehead. As I rose to my feet, I stared deeply at my child, thinking to myself that maybe I'm holding on to Ron for myself more than I am for her. Damn, what's a sista to do?

KIM

Malcolm is at football practice. I've got an hour before I pick him up, so I might as well do some grocery shopping. I swear that son of mine eats like a horse. An hour seemed like ten minutes as I stood in the Kroger's self check out line trying to hurry and get out of there. My watch read 2:55 p.m. and my son gets out at 3:05.

As I pulled up to his school, there he was talking to a group of girls. He noticed me and came to the car.

"Hey Mom," he said, leaning over and kissing me on the cheek.

"Hi baby." Looking back at the group of girls, I asked Malcolm, "Are those girls in your class?"

He smirked and said, "No, they're seniors."

Malcolm is very handsome and mature for his age. He looks so much like his father, Joseph. He and I went to school together. We were the idea couple. He was the quarterback on the football team and I was the reigning high school singles tennis champion at the peak of my game. We both had scholarships to further our academic as well as our athletic dreams.

But then I found out I was pregnant right after graduation. I was supposed to be going off to Spelman College, and him, off to Morehouse.

I remember it like it was yesterday. I was brushing my teeth and all of a sudden, I turned to the toilet throwing up.

With prom, graduation, and college on my agenda, I hadn't had a chance to think about the period I had missed. I was so sick that day that I went straight to the clinic. I thought they would give me some medicine and I'd be on my way. Instead, I got, *"Did you know you are pregnant?"*

I remember walking out of the clinic in a daze. I called Joseph from the pay phone. As soon as he picked up, he started jabbering about how cool it's going to be with him at Morehouse and myself right down the road at Spelman. He was so excited. I hated to break the news to him.

"I got something to tell you, and I need to see you right now."

We met at the park around the corner from my house. Before I could even get it out, he guessed it. Joseph knew me so well. He knew my cycle better than I did! We sat in silence for what seemed like an eternity. He stepped up and decided he wasn't leaving me here with a baby. Joseph decided we would make our lives in Chicago, where we grew up.

I asked about abortion, but he wasn't trying to hear that. He didn't believe in it. He ended up getting a job at the Chrysler Belvedere plant through his Mom. She was some kind of union big shot.

We leased a two bedroom apartment in Elmhurst at the Butterfield Towers. That wasn't the most convenient commute for Joseph to get to work, topping out at about one hour a day there and back. But he did it so that he could take care of me and Malcolm.

You know its funny how you really don't know a person until you live with them, but I'll get to that later.

As we arrived home, Malcolm helped me carry the groceries in the house. I looked at him and thought how he reminds me so much of his Dad. That thought quickly dissipated with a sour taste forming in mouth.

What I thought I Wanted

I'm hoping my son doesn't inherit some of the less valued traits his father has. Lord, what I learned about Joseph during our brief time living together turned my world upside down.

Chapter 4

STACY

I pulled the vanity mirror over the sun visor down to check myself out at the stop light, and I had to give it to myself.

"Gurlll, you looking good!"

I'm on my way to Mitch's house. He lives in Canton which is about 30 minutes from where I stay.

I can't lie, sometimes it does get scary coming over here. That's why I got my CCW and a 9mm. I don't want to hurt nobody, but I will protect myself.

Mitch and I have been messing around for some years now. I don't tell Amber or the rest of my girls, but he and I got history.

I've been pregnant by him twice. The twisted part is that it was me wanting to keep those babies. One time I waited almost too long to have an abortion on purpose. I was four months, going on five. I had to go in the hospital for that one. No clinic would touch me. Plus, wouldn't you know it…his old ass got me pregnant with twins.

While my girls thought I was gone to Hawaii for a week, I was really up in the hospital getting rid of something I wanted so desperately to keep. Mitch was firm in his stance. He wasn't having anything come back and touch his beloved wife, Jude.

What could I say? I mean I knew the situation going in. I knew my place, and it wasn't first.

Anyways, I started to get depressed as I turned down his block. I pulled the mirror down one more time for a quick check, and thought about how I had everybody fooled; Mitch, my girls, shit, even my Mom! That's right, everybody except myself. Truth is I love him. But days like this make me paranoid. That's all I need is his wife to come home or something.

He does all these wonderful things that most of these young guys don't. I bet when I get in the house he will have a bubble bath with candles. Yeah, that Mitch is a smooth mutha fuckah.

He'll bathe me down and slowly lotion me up. Then he'll put his sexual skills on and please me to the highest level. To top if off, he'll drop $1000.00 on me before I walk out the door. Even if I say no, he'll insist I take it. He always tells me I'm his baby and he's going to take care of me.

When we first started messing around, I was in debt higher than a thong at amateur night inside of 'Hot Tamales' strip club! My car was repossessed and he straightened it all out for me. Now my credit has made a 360° turn. I've learned a lot from him. That's why I guess I can't have a man. Well not a full-time man anyway, because if Mitch needs me, I'm there.

I parked my car in front of the neighbor's house and walked up the sidewalk to the door and there he was. I never have to ring the doorbell. He's always there waiting for me.

Mitch is in his mid-fifties, but he could pass for early forties. He's tall, like I like em' and is in excellent shape. His mocha brown skin is wrapped over a chiseled chest and six pack. He has the salt and pepper look going on. He's always clean shaven and his hair cut is always tight.

I've never dated a man so well groomed. Ladies, I must confess, the package he has in them drawls is like the difference between a regular meal at McDonald's or the Super sized meal!

"Hey Mitch," I said as I entered his home.

"Hey babydoll, come on in. I got your water ready. You want to eat first or do you want me to bathe you first?"

I thought for a second and then responded, "I'll eat first."

He had prepared shrimp Alfredo and broccoli with some garlic bread. We drank a couple of glasses wine and then it was bath time. I went upstairs and got into the water.

After he cleaned the kitchen, he joined me. He washed every inch of my body. Mitch dried me off and massaged me all over with lotion. He kissed every inch of my body that his hands explored.

As I rested back on the bed, he spread my legs to find that one part of me that stayed wet, no matter how many times he dried me off. As he touched my wetness with one hand, he rubbed that bulge in those silk pajama pants with the other.

Mitch knew what he had, and brandished it like the 'weapon' it was. I loved to remove his pants slowly, just to look at his 'manhood' standing at attention. Only to have it look right back at me! But before he would allow that masterpiece into my overflow, he would drink from 'her', letting his tongue and lips splash all over my wetness.

The way he used his tongue was like Mozart conducting his finest symphony. When he had me at the point of climax, just like a symphony building you up to a beautiful ending, Mitch looked onto my face to verify my complete satisfaction. Just as any good composer would do. Whoa, I tell you, that man had me in goose bumps already!

As my eyes again came focused on that big, juicy, mocha brown bone, all I could say to myself was "Damn! I'm lucky." When he laid it on me I felt that beautiful piece of God's creation enter into me, and all I could think about in my head was "SUPER SIZE ME!!!!!"

AMBER

I got to T.G.I. Friday's about 6pm, and went to the bar to have a seat. The bartender asked, "What can I get for you?"

"I'll have an apple martini," I replied.

Ameri walked up just as I ordered and said to me in his raspy voice, "How you doing babygirl? You looking good."

"Thank you, so do you." I smiled with every word that fell from my lips.

He smelled so good. As we munched on an appetizer and enjoyed our drinks, we talked about plant life. We laughed and really enjoyed each others company. We discussed his two sons and his relationship with their mother.

She was his high school sweetheart and they ended up getting married. He says after the second baby, their relationship changed dramatically.

He explained, "She just seemed to grow distant toward me. She stopped keeping herself up and never wanted to go back to work. Don't get me wrong Amber, I know post partum depression is real, but I've tried getting her psychological help. I even went to the gym with her, still nothing seemed to work."

As I was listening to him, I thought about the countless other men that have claimed trouble in a relationship, only to get 'some' from another woman. Funny, listening to Ameri, I believed him and even felt bad for him.

I finally asked, "So what's going on with you two now?"

He paused for a moment and let out a sigh, "Well, we are over. All we have are our kids. I've moved with my brother, but still spend a great deal of time with my boys."

Listening to him talk about his kids, I had to admit, the thought of a man with kids was pretty frightening. I mean, I don't have any children.

It's something about him that has my interest though. A part of me wants to get closer and know more about him.

Finally I ask, "So, you two are separated?"

He looked at me with a quizzical look on his face and answered, "Yes, if we were together, I wouldn't be sitting here with you. Look Amber, I love my children. I will do whatever I can for them. I haven't been dating anyone, but when I saw you that night it was something about you. I am not asking you for anything but your time. I really want to get to know you."

29

I felt the sincerity in his voice and smiled, "I would like that too."

Our first date was cool. We had good conversation, the best I've had with any man in a long time. Even though Ameri works at the plant, he is an Apprentice Electrician. He does electrical work on the side. Now that's what I'm talking about, a man with a legitimate hustle.

I told him about how I wanted to go back to school, but don't have the drive to just do it.

He touched my hand and said, "Well, if it's an extra push you need, then I'll be here to give it to you."

As he was saying that to me looking in my eyes, all I could think was, 'man those eyes are sexy.'

After about two hours, his phone vibrated. He took it off his hip and looked at it. He placed it back on his side, and we continued to talk. After we finished our drinks, he paid for everything and we proceeded to the parking lot.

He grabbed my hands and said, "I would really like to see you again. I feel a definite connection between us."

I didn't want to seem to desperate or excited, so I calmly said, "Well, just call me."

After a seductive kiss on the cheek, he opened my car door for me and shut it like a gentleman.

I rolled my window down and told him with a playful smile, "See you later."

He smiled back and gave me the same, "See you later."

As I pulled out of my parking space, he walked over to a black Tahoe with spinners and got in. I waved one last time and pulled off. Driving home, I thanked God for letting me have a nice date. I can't wait to see what's to come with Mr. Handsome.

LISA

Damn! It's 3am. I know it can't be nobody else ringing my bell but Ron. He's been blowing up my cell and home phone for days.

Ron doesn't care about nobody but himself. He knows I have to be up in two hours to get Simone to the babysitter in order to be at work on time. He's horrible at times. I haven't spoken to him since he stole my money.

Ron has done so much stuff to me. I've damn near been through it all. Other women calling me, abortions, his indiscretions with other women affecting my health, stealing, and even fighting to name a few.

Lord, I wish he would just leave us alone. It's not any use calling the police, because I've called them so much to this address, I think that got me on a 'don't even answer this call list.'

The knocking and bell ringing stopped. I'm glad it didn't wake Simone. As I sat up in my bed, I thanked GOD for giving me the strength not to answer the door or my phone for him. I was glad to have some peace. I was just hoping he wouldn't be outside when I left out for work.

It seemed like 5am came before I knew it. I got up and did my regular routine. Simone and I were dressed and out the door by 6am.

Right after I dropped her off at the babysitter, my cell phone started ringing. I knew by the Mary J. Blige, 'No more tears' ringtone, it was Ron. I didn't answer it, because I knew he wanted to argue and I had no patience for that drama. I just wasn't feeling it today.

Ron was the type of man that could drain your whole spirit, and I didn't feel like allowing myself to be drained. I punched into work with only ten minutes left before the bell rang.

My phone was vibrating on my hip like crazy. I began to work trying to keep my mind off the damn vibrating phone. I thought about getting my life together to provide a better upbringing for Simone.

My first break came and I went to sit down in the break room. Looking at the caller ID on my cell phone, it read *16 missed calls.*

I let out a loud sigh and dialed my voicemail only to hear, "You have seven new messages."

First message: "Hey Lisa this Ron, why you won't answer? Call me back."

Next message: a hang up.

Next message: "Damn Lisa, this some bullshit. I'm sorry for everything. Just call me back. I need you. I need Simone. I need to see y'all. Call me back."

Next message: "Lisa, come on girl. You know I can't take this shit! You and Simone the only thing I got good in my life. I can't live like this. I can't take you not speaking to me Lisa. Please, I'm begging you. Call me. Just let me hear your voice. I promise, I won't argue with you. I can't live without ya'll. If I can't have ya'll, I might as well not be here."

Ron tried that suicide stuff so many times. Usually it worked, but not this time. After I leave his ass alone, he always goes into 'I'm going to kill myself' mode.

I'm not breaking down for his ass this time.

Next message: "Baby, I'm sorry for putting you through everything."

I could hear his Mom in the background saying, "Ron baby, no! Don't do this Ron, please!"

He continued on, "Lisa I know I've done you wrong and you deserve better, but you just wouldn't give me one more chance…"

His Mom was getting louder, "Ron please! Baby!"

He starts to get more aggressive in his tone, "I told you I will **NOT** live without you."

I heard a click in the background and he continued, "All you had to do was sit down and talk to me. I just wanted to try and work things out between us but no, you've pushed me too far. I know you've never believed me when I said I won't live without you and Simone, well I hope you believe me now…I love you."

When he finished his sentence, I heard a gunshot and the phone drop. His Mom screamed, "No! Oh Lord no!"

The phone hung up. I was in a state of shock, with my ear still to the phone.

Next message: "Lisa, it's Gladys! Call me please!!!"

Next message: "Lisa, it's Gladys! Baby, Ron done shot himself and has been rushed to Receiving Hospital. It ain't looking good baby. It ain't looking good at all! Paramedics say he lost a lot of blood! Baby, please call me on his cell phone! I'm on my way to the hospital now!!!

After hearing that last message, I returned the cell phone to my side. I couldn't even get myself mentally prepared to call his Mom back. I sat in the break room in utter shock. I was speechless.

As I stood up from the table I felt weak and confused. All I could think was, *'He really did it…he really shot himself.'*

I finally snapped out of it and pulled my phone from my side racing out the break room door.

I called his Mom, "Hello, this is Lisa! I'm on my way."

I didn't even wait for a response. I hung up and moved quickly to gather my things. He's my child's father and I do love him. I've got to get out of here and get to that hospital!

What I thought I Wanted

<u>KIM</u>

I saw Lisa pass by my job with a dazed look on her face moving fast as hell! I called her name, but she didn't answer. I asked my co-worker, Brenda to watch my job for a minute.

I caught up with her and asked, "Hey girl what's wrong?"

Tears were streaming down her face. She blurted out, "Kim, Ron shot himself."

I was so shocked that I could barely even speak, "What happened? Why?"

She was so upset. She told me she was trying to leave him alone and hadn't been talking or seeing him for weeks. It started with him at her house last night and ended this morning with him in the hospital.

I told Lisa not to worry about Simone, and that I'd pick her up and take her home with me. I found her supervisor and explained to him the situation. Lisa gathered her work bag and rushed out of the plant doors.

I told Amber and Stacy what had happened. After work, I dashed over to the babysitter's house to pick up Simone. She was my Goddaughter. The babysitter was Malcolm's babysitter when he was younger.

As I approached the front door, there she was standing in front of it with a look of disgust on her face.

"Hey, Ms. Mary. I'm here to pick up Simone."

"I know chile'. Lisa called me," Ms. Mary said.

Ms. Mary was an older woman with streaks of grey shooting through hair. She had that accent that let you know she was a southern girl.

As we entered her home, she said, "Boy, that Ron is some piece of work. Best thing he ever did was make that beautiful little girl .Yeah baby, Lisa called not too long ago and ain't have no word on him yet. She said the doctors said he shot himself in the chest area. Umph! Baby, if you ask me, he shoulda put the

gun to his head if he really wanted to kill himself. That boy ain't
really want to kill himself. If he did, he woulda put it to his head.
He somethin' else. He don't want nothin' out of life but to hang
on to Lisa and leech off her. Just like he did and still doin' his
mama."

Only pausing to catch her breath, she continued with,

"You know me and Gladys go way back, since our young
days in Mississippi."

I had heard the story of how Ms. Mary knew Ron's
mother many times. She told it so often, because she hated to see
the way Ron did Lisa. Like most, these ladies migrated to the
North once they grew up.

Ms Mary sat down at the kitchen table and rocked back
and forth.

"Well, enough about that chile'. Simone is in my bed
taking a nap. How's my boy?"

My face lit up as she referred to my son.

"He's fine Ms Mary."

She smiled back, "That's good. He don't come see me
anymore. You don't ever hear from his daddy, do you?"

My disposition quickly changed.

"No, Ms. Mary and I hope I don't ever. I don't need any
trouble from him. He's taken me through enough. That chapter
of my life is over and I pray it stays in the past. As long as
Malcolm is okay, I'm okay."

Ms Mary always asks about him, or rather when she
thought I was in a decent mood. As I reflected back in my mind I
thought about all I'd been through with him. I'd confided in Ms.
Mary and thanks to her and the grace God, I made it through
some very hard times. I guess that's why I hate to see Lisa go
through this now.

Ms. Mary had a tendency to keep asking questions. I
guess she figured she was old enough to ask anybody anything
she wanted, if she wanted to know. My face clearly showed her I

wasn't interested in discussing Malcolm's dad, but she asked another question anyway.

"Have you ever told Lisa bout you and Joseph?"

"No, Ms. Mary. I haven't told her. I don't talk about that with anyone and I'd appreciate you not talking about it with anyone either."

She patted me on my hand and reassured me that she hadn't.

"Calm down baby. I never told it and I won't tell it. You like a daughter to me."

I relaxed a little and let the tension escape my muscles.

"I'm sorry Ms. Mary."

She stood up and stretched her arms out and I embraced her hug.

She said softly, "Baby, I love you and would never do anything to hurt you."

Just as we released each other from a much needed hug, Simone appeared in the kitchen.

"Hey, Auntie Kim. You picking me up today?"

"Hey baby girl. I sure am" I said.

Ms. Mary and I smiled at one another, before I looked at Simone.

"Well, baby girl, I guess you spending the rest of the evening with Auntie. What will it be for dinner tonight; pizza or McDonald's?"

Simone cheered, "Pizza, pizza."

Ms. Mary grabbed my hand as we were walking out of the door and whispered to me, "Baby, what you went through is nothin' short of amazin'. I know what happened is hard to talk about, but don't let what happen to you happen to Lisa. Just think bout it baby, you can be a testimony and a blessing to that girl."

I knew Ms. Mary was right. With tears in my eyes I looked at Simone and then back at Ms. Mary and said, "You're right Ms. Mary."

I walked to my car and opened the door for Simone. I looked at Ms. Mary again and said, "It's hard to talk about what you've tried so hard to forget."

LISA

I've been sitting here in the waiting room for what feels like days. His mom has been crying so much. I feel worse for her than I do for him.

I guess because she has already lost one son. Ron's older brother James was killed two years ago in a shooting at a club. The shooting was over some girl he was dating. Turns out the girl's ex-boyfriend was obsessed with her and when he found out who James was, he followed them to the club and killed both of them.

I've been trying to console Gladys as much as I can. She's just been sitting down with her head in her lap.

Finally, she looked up and told me, "Baby, Ron really loves you. When he makes it through this, please try and work it out. I can't take losing another child. I know Ron has his faults, every man does. Just promise me that you will try and work it out. Can you do that for me?"

I responded with a blank stare on my face. I couldn't believe she would use the guilt trip on me.

The doctor came out to the waiting area and asked, "Family for Ronald Sims?"

His mother jumped up and replied, "Yes, I'm his mother."

The doctor introduced himself and began explaining Ron's status.

"I'm Dr. Graham, your son is stable. He did puncture one lung, and subsequently suffered what is called traumatic pneumothorax. In short, his left lung collapsed. However, we were able to repair it. He's very lucky that he was transported to the hospital as quickly as he was. He's resting comfortably now. The next 48 to 72 hours are very important. Once he is out of the woods, he will have to undergo psychiatric evaluation. Because of the nature of this incident, it is a must."

As Dr. Graham's words registered, his mother realized her son would be okay and eagerly asked to see him.

"Where is he? May I visit him now?"

"Sure, follow me."

She looked at me and said, "Lisa, you coming?"

I nervously responded, "Yes."

When we walked into his room, he seemed to be sleeping. We stood at his beside in complete silence. All you could hear was the machines in the room working to keep him breathing and stable.

Ms. Gladys kneeled down by his bedside and began to pray aloud,

"Father, God, thank you for sparing my son's life. He's all I have now. Lord, keep his mind and make him strong."

She reached over and grabbed my hand, *"Lord, heal Lisa and Ron's relationship. Help Lisa to see the good my boy has in him and how much he loves her and Simone. Work it out for them Lord."*

I can't lie, part of me wanted to snatch my hand away, but I knew it would hurt her feelings. While she was praying for us, I was questioning if God wanted me to be with Ron. In light of him doing this, I wondered was this a sign for me to stay away or try and work us out. Being with Ron is like having two kids. His mom has spoiled him and he really wears me down. This time I was really moving on without him, and now he pulls this stunt, damn.

I was thinking about his mother's request and her prayers when I asked myself, "Why me?"

As soon as that thought ran through my mind, Ron began to wake up.

He was stirring and managed to groan a little. His mom rose to her feet and let my hand go to hold on to his with both hands.

"Hey, baby! Momma loves you," she said with tears in her eyes.

By his groans you could tell he was in pain. Then he looked past her and our eyes met. I smiled awkwardly. I felt so much emotion at that time. I was choked up at the thought of Simone's father dying because of me.

His mom moved closer to her son's face.

"Baby, Momma gonna be right here by your side. You really scared us. You know we love you and don't want to lose you. Yep, we all gone move on from this and be one happy family."

My emotions quickly changed from nervousness to anger in 0.01 seconds! How can she expect us to be one big happy family? I mean, I do still love Ron, but I can't take care of him.

As she continued with the 'us and we' conversation, I couldn't help but get pissed at how she was trying to make decisions for me and my child. As I stared into Ron's eyes, he kind of nodded 'yes' to his mother as she talked.

Listening to her had me ready to leave this room and this hospital. Just as I had made up my mind to get the hell out of this place, his Mom turned to me and pleaded, "Baby, let me get out the way so you can talk to Ron."

Now I was on the spot, so as she moved out the way, I moved closer toward him. I spoke to him with confused emotions.

"Hi, Ron."

Although he couldn't talk, I could see the happiness in his face to see me. I smiled at him wondering in my head, 'why did he do this'. I held his hand and I could almost feel he loved me. All this was too much to bear and I was ready to get out of here.

What I thought I Wanted

I looked at him with compassion and said, "Well, you need to rest. I've got to go get Simone. I'm sure she is wondering what happened to me by now. I will check on you tomorrow, after work."

I turned to Ms. Gladys and gave her a hug, "I will call you later."

She smiled with tear filled eyes and sobbed, "Ok, baby. Kiss my grandbaby for me."

As I walked out that hospital that evening, I was consumed with so many emotions. I hate to say it, but guilt was one of them. I felt bad that I didn't open the door for him last night or answer the phone this morning. I felt like I'm trapped in something I will never get out of. I know Ron, and once he's able to talk he's going to remind me how he tried to kill himself for me for the rest of my life.

I just don't know what to do. I'm so confused right now. I'm going by Kim's house to pick up my baby and go home. I don't want to talk about what he did or what I'm going to do.

After getting in my car and turning the key in the ignition, the radio popped on and Syleena Johnson's 'Guess What' was on the radio. Listening to Syleena tell that brother off was just what I needed to hear.

I found myself singing alone, popping my fingers and driving down I-75 toward I-696 to pick my baby up. Man, at that moment, I felt like Syleena was my best friend and we had been through the same things. As the song ended, I wondered what she would do in my shoes.

I thought back to his Mom's prayer and on a lot of the things Ron put me through. Finally I told myself, if there is such a thing as hell on earth, this nightmare I'm in may very well be it. I hope I wake up soon.

Chapter 5

STACY

I've been trying to be there for Lisa. After that shit Ron did last week, my girl just hasn't been herself. I guess I can't blame her. I know she feels sorry for him and blames herself, but I hope she don't go back to him.

I'm so glad it's the Labor Day weekend. I don't have to go to work Monday, so I can hang out all weekend. My union steward, Alonzo wants me to come and walk down Woodward with the rest of the unions Monday morning for the annual Labor Day Parade. I don't know about getting up that early if I don't have to, a girl has to get her beauty rest some time!

Alonzo or as everyone calls him Zo, is my union steward and has gotten me out of some messed up situations at work. Zo can work his tongue like a snake charmer on a snake. I know that if I march on Monday, we getting' buckwild afterwards. What bitch do you know who don't like a man that knows how to use his tongue? Plus he got a body!

Anyways, after I finish getting my nails and toes done at Greenfield Plaza, I need to hurry up and get home. Overtime at work has been a little slow, but I'm still making my paper.

My 'little' friend Mike is coming to pick me up around 7pm. He's cool, but I really don't like short guys. He's taller than me, but I usually like my men 6 feet and over. Mike is about 5' 10". Plus, my heart is with Mitch.

Speaking of Mitch, he is out of town for the Labor Day weekend doing the family thang. That's the down side to dating a married man you love. You got to know your place. But I don't let it phase me, it's plenty of brothers out here that will take a sister out and spend a little money. Like my friend, Mike.

"Ma, answer the door," I hollered out from upstairs when I heard the doorbell ring for the second time. I glanced at the clock on my nightstand and it read 7pm. Mike is always on time.

He was standing at the front door talking to my mother as I walked down the steps. His short ass really knows how to dress. He had a sky blue linen two-piece short set on with some Kenneth Cole shoes. He wore an expensive looking Rolex on one wrist with a diamond bracelet on the other. Mike rocked some Cartier frames and a three carat diamond earring in his ear. And to add insult to injury, his cologne would have a bitch on instant overflow from his scent! Dayum!

"Dang Ma, you acting like *you* want him or something. You mighty close," I said teasing her.

"Girl, if I wanted him, I could have him. Ain't that right Mike?"

He just grinned as I gave him an innocent mean mug. My mother was just an older version of me. Most times people thought she was my sister. The only difference was that she was into younger men, and well, I'm into older gentleman.

Mike and I headed out the door when I stopped him and asked where we were going. He walked in front of me to open my door, but still didn't answer my question.

He pulled on the door handle to his red with black trim, 1970 Boss 302 Mustang. It was a bad ass ride, and I loved riding in it almost more than I did him. I got in with pride. He only drove it in the summer up until Labor Day, so you won't see it on the streets again until next summer.

He closed the door after making sure I was in, and went to the driver's side. Once in he told me we were going to Sinbad's downtown. I loved seafood, and he could tell I approved by the way I glanced over at him, giving him a seductive wink.

We looked good together. His caramel skin coated over that body builder's body, next to my chocolate skin and voluptuous body. Whoa! The thought alone makes me slippery between the thighs.

The truth is that Mike is a really nice guy. I know he wants more than what I give him. I just ain't ready for a commitment; at least not with him. Don't get me wrong, he would do anything for me, but the sex ain't hittin' like with Mitch. Mitch is just the total package. Maybe it's because he's older.

When we arrived at Sinbad's, the valet opened my door and Mike collected the ticket. I know he's checking me out in this fitted skirt I got on. He loves when I wear something tight to show off my figure. Mike has no problems when other guys look at me.

The hostess seated us at a nice table near the window. The view of the Detroit River along with the lit candle on the table was setting the perfect mood.

After we placed our order and our glasses of wine arrived, Mike took a sip and asked, "Stacy, aren't you tired of just dating?"

He almost made me choke. I really didn't want to talk about this. I am tired of dating, but what I want is unavailable.

I answered back, "Yeah, I'm tired…but I don't know if I'm really ready to settle down."

He looked at me for a moment, and then reached for my hand, "Look Stacy, we been messing around for over a year now. I'm thirty-two years old. I got myself together, my own house, 401k plan, and a lot of love to give a wife and family. I really care about you. I don't care about what nobody says about you, I'm into you."

When he made that comment, I knew what he was talking about. Some of those hatin' ass hoes at the plant be trying to get Mike to mess with them, and he won't do it. They tell him how I'm a hoe and messing with a whole lot of guys at the plant, especially the loan shark, Mitch.

One thing I can say about Mike, he don't give a damn what nobody got to say about me. He never changes and he always tells me who's talking about me.

I squeezed his hand and gave him a sincere response.

"Mike, I know you have feelings for me. I got feelings for you too, but I don't know if a relationship between you and I could work."

He looked with concern, "Why do you say you don't know if it will work? Is it because of Mitch?"

"No, it's not because of Mitch!"

This is the part where the sincerity faded and the lies came out.

"Look Stacy, I know you care about him, but he is a married man. My dad worked with Mitch for twenty-two years. My dad told me Mitch has been with Jude for over thirty years and he is not going to ever leave her. I hope it's not because of him that you won't give us a shot. Give yourself a shot at having a lasting relationship with someone who truly loves you. Because I do love you Stacy and I feel you deserve a man that can give you all of him."

Oh my God, he said he loves me. He loves me? I don't think I've ever heard a man say he loves me, unless we're fucking. At that moment he made my heart melt. I looked into those hazel eyes and knew he meant every word he was saying. I was speechless.

"Mike, I don't know what to say..."

That hard exterior I had was getting softer by the minute. All I could think about was Mitch though. This is crazy. A man is pouring his heart out to me and all I can think about is a married man.

The waiter returned with our entrees just as Mike was about to continue. I couldn't concentrate on eating. We ate in silence for a few minutes and finally, Mike put his fork down and said, "I don't want to scare you Stacy. I just couldn't hide

45

my feelings any longer. This mode we are in is just not enough for me, but I don't want to lose you. We don't have to talk about this anymore right now. You were my friend first and we grew from there."

I looked into his handsome face and said, "Mike you know so much about me. You've been my confidante when I couldn't confide in anyone else. You never judge me and have always been there for me…just give me some time to digest all of this. You've given me a lot to think about. I'm not saying that I don't want to try. I'm just saying, I need some time to think out my feelings and emotions. Ok?"

He didn't hesitate, "Ok."

We finished dinner with light conversation about the Detroit Lions, plant life, and my favorite subject sex. After Mike opened up to me like that, I was ready to be with him. His lovemaking skills could be polished up, but tonight it didn't matter. He opened his heart to me and that was a turn on in itself. Yeah, we had to work on the bedroom skills. He had the right equipment, but the rhythm was off. We seemed to be listening to two different songs when we had sex. I was listening to Between the Sheets by the Isley Brothers and he was listening to 'Push it' by Salt & Pepa.

Right now, my juices were flowing for Mike. He knew that look I had in my eye. He paid the waiter and we exited the building.

As we headed down Jefferson Avenue to I-75, he reached over and rubbed my thigh.

"You going home with me?"

I grabbed his hand on my thigh and put it up my skirt in my panties so his fingers could feel my wetness, and asked "What you think?"

He took his hand from under my skirt, and sucked each finger and said, "I guess that's a yes."

We got to his home in Warren, in no time flat. After we pulled in the garage, we started getting it on before he even opened the door to the house. Man, he was a beast tonight! After a few minutes of kissing and feeling, he got the key in the door and we headed straight for his bedroom. He ripped my tight shirt off my body and started sucking my breasts.

Oh! That shit felt so good! I took his shirt off and began to suck his nipples. He pulled my skirt up and snatched my panties off. I like that aggressive shit. Tonight we were fucking, fuck that love making shit! He picked me up and sat me on top of his dresser, got down on his knees and began to feast on my warm, wet center. Before I knew it, I was reaching my climax and exploded like a volcano.

He stood up and I jumped down off the dresser and pushed him toward the bed. After an orgasm like that, the only thing that could satisfy me further was some dick. He fell back on the bed and I pulled his shorts and underwear off at the same time. I couldn't take my eyes off that dick. Looking at it made my mouth water. I sucked it like I was trying to get to the center of a tootsie pop as he moaned with ecstasy.

Finally I had returned the favor as he came in my mouth and all over my breasts. He stayed hard and I then mounted him. I rode that dick like a jockey in the Kentucky Derby! As we moaned together, Mike grabbed my ass and maneuvered his massive dick inside of me. Then he came with that freaky talk, "You like this? You like this shit? This is how you want it?"

I couldn't believe Mike was fucking me like this. I was reaching my climax for the second time, and I started screaming, "Yes Daddy, give it to me!"

We came together and I collapsed on top of him. I rested on top of his chest, feeling totally satisfied and free. As he slept, I laid there and thought back to what he said to me at dinner. Mike told me I deserved someone who could give me all of themselves. He felt I deserved better. A tear streamed down my face, and the last thought I had before drifting off to sleep was why didn't I think I deserved better?

AMBER

It was Saturday afternoon and I had just hung up the phone from Ameri. We've been talking more often these past weeks. I'm really feeling him. He seems to be a dedicated father. He has his kids involved in a lot of after school activities.

Mike and I have been out a couple of times now, but nothing in particular. I guess we are in the 'getting to know each other' phase. Oh well, I'm down to see where it takes us.

I'm not use to a brother moving this slow. He told me he doesn't just want a sexual relationship, so he is taking his time and getting to know me.

His favorite phrase is, "Let's stimulate each others mind, before we stimulate each others bodies." I don't know about him, but I'm already stimulated.

So I made up my mind. Tonight was going to be the night the 'magic was going to happen'. We have a date at 8pm. Up until now, I haven't been to his place and he hasn't been to mine.

He's coming over for the first time and I got dinner already started. My chicken parmesan is in the oven, spaghetti with marinara sauce is on the stove and a fresh roll of French bread is on the counter. I got some red and white wine in my wine cooler, with a tossed spinach salad and balsamic dressing.

Everything was going to be perfect. Dinner was done and I had time to soak in my whirlpool tub and then get fabulous. He would be here in less than two hours.

The kisses we've been sharing have been explosive, leaving me wanting more. I hope tonight we can stimulate our bodies. I mean, I don't sleep around, but my body needs some sexual healing. It's been a while since I've had some. I broke up with me ex about nine months ago. He didn't want nothing out of life, but to party all night and sleep all day. But that's enough about his trifling ass, my mind is locked on my big date with Ameri.

I'm ready to put the good girl in me to the side and bring out Ms. Bad Ass. I checked the dining room, it was flawless. I took a long look in the mirror and I was flawless as well. I had on a nice silk Gucci semi sheer blouse, opened just a little to show some cleavage, a pair of grey Gucci Bermudas, with my favorite black tall Gucci boots. And last but not least, I wore some vintage Gucci perfume to invigorate his sense of smell.

I took the chicken parmesan out of the stove and let it cool. It was thirty minutes until he was expected to arrive, and I was sitting back on the couch watching television. This gave me a chance to calm down and get my nerves together.

I'm nervous and excited all at the same time. I've been up since early this morning and was a little tired. Flicking through the channels, I settled on CSI. I figured I would watch that until he arrived.

Damn! I must have fallen asleep. My eyes focused on the clock on the wall, it read 10pm. Where is he? I checked my cell phone, no new messages and no missed calls on the caller ID. I hope something hasn't happened to him. He's usually on time or calls if he is running late.

I called his cell phone, it went straight to voicemail, *"Ameri, this is Amber. I don't know what happened to you. I hope you are alright. I'm worried about you, call me. This is not like you."*

I called his cell phone at least twenty times in the next two hours. I even watched the 11 o'clock news to see if any fatal shootings or car crashes had occurred. I finally changed my clothes and lied down in the bed around midnight. I was so worried. I called Kim, and told her what happened.

"Maybe something happened with one of his kids. When you have children, anything is possible. Try not to worry Amber.

Did you try calling his house?" Kim said trying to calm me down.

"No, he doesn't have a regular house phone. He uses his cell phone all the time."

She suggested, "Well, you could ride by his house. But it is really too late for you to be riding out from downtown to Westland at 12 o'clock at night."

"You're right and I couldn't ride out there anyway. I haven't been over there yet. This was supposed to be his first time at my house. I'm really worried Kim."

Kim sympathized with me, "I know Amber, but all you can do is wait."

She went on to tell me that Lisa was going to the hospital to see Ron everyday, also that she's been so depressed since he tried to kill himself.

I hated what Lisa was going through. She just can't seem to get away from Ron. As soon as she seems to move forward, he does something to make her take three steps back. Back to him that is.

I made a mental note to check on Lisa later on today.

"Thanks for listening Kim. I'll let you know what happens, love you."

"Love you too girl," Kim closed the call.

I was awakened out of my sleep at 2am by the phone ringing.

"Hey baby. Sorry I couldn't call earlier, but my son A.J. had an asthma attack and I took him to the hospital," he explained.

"Is he alright?"

"Yeah baby. He's doing fine. His mother is at the hospital with him now. The doctors decided to keep him overnight. I was supposed to go to work this morning, but I don't think I can make it. Can I still come by and see you for a little while?"

I smiled at the thought he still wanted to see me. I quickly answered, "Yeah. You have the directions and the address. Come on over."

I hung up the phone and darted into the bathroom to freshen up. I took a quick shower and brushed my teeth.

Getting clean was the easy part, but choosing which panties to wear became a task in itself. After looking at about 25 pair, I finally decided to not wear any at all. That's right, my birthday suit would be the showcase of the morning! Sike! I ended up putting on my red Vickie Secrets pajama pants...I'm always a lady first!

The gatehouse called to let me know Ameri was here so I unlocked my front door. He knocked and I yelled for him to come right in. He looked wonderful. He came straight up to me and wrapped his arms around me. It felt so good and so right.

I reluctantly pulled back from his embrace and asked, "How are you?"

"I'm okay baby, just tired and hungry."

I felt sorry for my baby.

"Well, I can either make you some breakfast or you can have the dinner you missed last night."

"I didn't eat all day because I knew I was having dinner with you. So I think I'll have what I missed last night."

When he smiled at me, my mind went straight to the gutter. Oblivious to him, he missed more than dinner.

I told him to have a seat in the living room as I went into the kitchen. I warmed his plate up and set it on the table. He complimented my place settings and then excused himself to wash his hands. I was impressed when I saw him say his grace before eating. Now that was something you don't see every man do, pray over their food before they eat it.

After Ameri ate, we sat on the living room sofa and watched an old movie together. During small talk, Ameri put his head in my lap. I know I was supposed to be consoling him and feeling sorry for him, but all I could think about was sex. I was so horny, the warmth of his head on my legs was making me wet. My nipples were aching for some attention.

He fell asleep in my lap and I didn't have the nerve to try and seduce him. So eventually, I laid my head back on the sofa and fell asleep as well.

I was awakened by his lips touching mine. It was the sweetest kiss ever. He kissed me slow and passionately. I couldn't believe this was happening. He gently touched my breasts and my aching started to be soothed.

Ameri unbuttoned my top and exposed my breasts. He kissed and sucked them oh so gently. Part of me wanted to rush the moment, but the attention my body was getting was long overdue. He touched me the right way in all the right places.

He took his shirt off to reveal a magnificent upper body. I couldn't wait to see his pants come off. I stood up from the sofa and he looked up at me with his seductive eyes. He gently pulled my silk pajama pants down. He examined every inch of me that was revealed as if he was studying it for a test. That's what I'm talking about ladies, a man with a brain who also knows how to use it!

He began to kiss my stomach and thighs. I couldn't take it any longer. I helped him take his pants off to expose his manhood. I aggressively pushed him back down on the sofa and mounted him.

For the next forty-five minutes our bodies made music. He made me feel so good, I never wanted to let go. Two climaxes later, we lied back on the sofa, both exhausted and happy.

He looked deeply in my eyes, "Amber, I really tried not to take it to this level, but when I woke up and saw you sleeping, I couldn't resist kissing you. I just couldn't help myself. I hope you are not angry with me?"

The fact that he considered my feelings had me going, "Ameri, I'm not mad at you. I wanted you just as much as you wanted me. If you wouldn't have taken it there, I probably would have."

He reached over to the end table and grabbed his watch, he said, "I've got to get back to the hospital. I wish I could spend more time with you, but I have to go."

I wasn't very happy to hear that, but I understood. I showed him to the shower and we got in together. Things got hot and steamy in there and we indulged our bodies one last time before he left for the hospital. As Ameri walked out my door, he promised to call me later. I watched him walk away and I thought to myself, "I wonder are you the one I'll spend the rest of my life with?"

<u>KIM</u>

I am so tired. Staying up last night talking to Amber on the phone was exhausting. I hope she's alright. I've been calling her house all morning and haven't got an answer yet. Well, I guess I'll get my butt up and hit the gym. I've been doing real good with my diet and exercising three times a week.

If I hurry up I can get there by noon and be out by one. I love going to the gym. It gives me an opportunity to unwind from all my stress.

My girls always think I got it together, but I don't. I've been trying to be the big sister for all of them. Out of all three of them, Lisa and I are the closest. I really feel sorry for her. She's beating herself up these days because of what Ron's grown ass did to himself. She's taking all the blame, thinking she should've at least tried to talk to him when he attempted to reach out to her.

I've been there and done that. Ron reminds me so much of Joseph. They don't look alike, but they sure have a lot of the same ways.

What I thought I Wanted

I got to the gym in fifteen minutes. I went upstairs to the cardio equipment to do my hour on the treadmill. As I got into my brisk walk, the finest personal trainer ever walked past my machine.

He had an almond complexion, was muscular and cut up, like a professional body builder. He smiled at me as he walked past; his teeth were perfect and white.

I was caught by surprise when he spoke to me. I almost fell checking him out. I haven't dated in a long time, so looking is all I do.

Since moving to Michigan and away from Joseph, I swore I would never let any other man affect Malcolm and I like he did.

Amber and Stacy were always trying to get me to go out with someone. As they put it, "I need some you know what in my life." Those girls don't know me. I had a pair of C batteries and a vibrator that did the job when I had some sexual tension I needed to release. But who am I fooling? It's still not like having someone to touch and caress your body.

I continued on the treadmill and made a mental list of everything I had to do, which included homework for anatomy and physiology. I had to get Malcolm some more cleats for football, and check on Lisa. She hasn't been communicating with me like she normally does.

An hour later I was done. As I was walking out the door, that same personal trainer was standing at the information booth. Before I could pass him to exit the building, he yelled out, "Miss, may I have just a moment of your time?"

I walked over and waited for his sales pitch.

"I'm new to the gym and couldn't help but notice you upstairs on the treadmill. I apologize if this is inappropriate."

I guess he couldn't help but notice me since I almost broke my neck looking at him.

"I would like to give you my card, not to set up a free first session with me, but to see if you would like to go out sometime. I've been watching you for quite a while and didn't have the nerve to speak up. But I couldn't let you go by this time without opening my mouth. Here is my card, please call me if you would like to go out."

"Thanks. I'll do that," I said as I took the card and put it in my purse.

I got to my car and pulled it out to read the name, "Alan Williams, personal trainer." But just as I have done every man that has tried to approach me, I dismissed the thought. I put the card in my purse, and pulled out the parking lot.

Since I was already on I-75, I decided to take a ride on the east side to check on Lisa. My cell phone started ringing, and as usual, I can't find anything in this purse of mine.

"Hello?" I answered when I finally found it.

"Hey girl, what's up?"

I laughed, "You know you are not right. I've been calling you all morning."

I could feel the happiness resonating from Amber's voice, "Maybe that's because I finally got some!"

I laughed in excitement with her. It had only been nine months for her, but way longer for me. At least one of us was satisfied.

She couldn't wait to give me the play by play. She was so excited, "Kim, girl, he was so damn sweet. He touched me and caressed me like I needed to be touched. He was so affectionate."

I couldn't help but ask, "What happened to him last night?"

"Girl, you were right. His son had an asthma attack and he had to take him to the hospital. He was supposed to go to work this morning, but he was too tired to make it. He asked if it was alright if he still came over. Of course I said yes and the rest was history."

I was a little bothered by him not at least calling Amber, but I guess she forgot all about that. Out of concern, I asked, "He left him at the hospital alone?"

"Nah girl, his son's mother came and she stayed there with him."

That was a little troubling to me, "Are they still together?"

"No mother Kim, they are not! They are legally separated. He stays with his brother and she is still in the house until the divorce is final."

"Well Amber, you be careful with that. You know some men will say they're separated and still be with that woman."

Amber smacked her lips, "Damn Kim, you sure know how to bring a sister down. As much as we have been going out and after last night, I hardly think he is lying."

"If I didn't love you, I wouldn't say anything. I don't know Ameri, but I know you and I only want the best for you."

She paused, "I know Kim. I'm sorry for getting mad. I know you're only looking out for me and I will be careful. What you about to get into?"

"I'm on my way over to Lisa's house. I haven't been able to reach her. Have you talked to her?"

"Nope. I tried to call her too, and didn't get any answer. You mind if I tag along?"

"No, I'll come by and pick you up and we can go together."

"Alright Kim, I'll be ready when you get here."

After I hung up the phone, my mind wandered to this Ameri. I hope he was on the up and up. Amber is a good girl and deserves a good guy. Sometimes she can be too trusting, like with the last fool she was dating. He turned out to be a real psycho.

Exiting I-75 and turning on to Jefferson Avenue, I thought for a brief minute about how empty my life was 'socially.' I used school, work, my son, and my friends to occupy all my time. Maybe I should take Amber and Stacy's advice and start dating. It's a thought. Maybe Mr. Williams could be my first date. Just maybe he could.

LISA

Who could be at my door? I looked out my living room curtains to see Kim and Amber standing on my porch. I let out a long sigh. I wasn't ready to face anybody. I opened the door, and put my game face on, "What's up ladies? What brings you by my way?"

I knew Kim would speak up first, "We've been trying to get in touch with you. Calling and leaving messages wasn't getting us anywhere, so we decided to drop by to see if you were okay. We were worried about you and Simone."

Before I could even respond, Ron called out from the bedroom, "Lisa, can you make me a sandwich? But this time put extra mayo on it and cut the crust off."

Amber and Kim looked at each other in surprise.

"Oh! We didn't know you had a house guest!" Amber said with sarcasm dripping from her words.

I asked them to have a seat in the kitchen, while I made Ron's sandwich.

"Look, he needed someone to be with him for a couple of days. His mother went to Mississippi for the Labor Day weekend and she asked if he could stay here. I couldn't say no. I mean, I don't want him to try this stunt again."

Ron yelled again, "Lisa, did you hear me? Why aren't you answering me?"

"I heard you Ron. Give me a minute!"

Simone came running from her room straight to Kim, giving her a big hug.

"Hi, Auntie Kim. Hi, Auntie Amber," my little bundle of joy said smiling from ear to ear.

She reminded me so much of my mother. Those eyes of hers were just like my mother's.

"Simone sweetie, take this sandwich to your daddy."

"Okay, Mommy."

She walked toward the back of the house, holding the plate with both hands, being real careful not to drop her daddy's sandwich. Simone disappeared, and I was met with a look from my two friends that was anything but friendly.

I quickly spoke up, "No ladies, we are not back together."

I sat down at my kitchen table and looked from left to right at the both of them.

"Truthfully, my feelings have really changed."

Amber loved to ask questions, "Changed how?"

"Well, last night he started rubbing and touching me. I didn't feel anything. It used to be a time when he could look at me and I wanted to take my clothes off and rape him. But now, it just ain't there."

I looked to Kim for words of inspiration. As usual she delivered. "Lisa, you can't make yourself still be in love with Ron. Despite what has happened, it doesn't take away all he has done. You can still be there for him and not with him."

While we were talking low, I was still afraid he would hear us, so a gestured for us to go out side. I hollered to the back of the house where Ron was, "Ron, I'm going to walk Amber and Kim outside. I'll be right back in."

While he hadn't asked who was in the house, I'm sure he knew it was one of my friends. Ron didn't like them and they didn't like him. He used to say they are what kept the wedge between us. They said he was a loser and I should leave him.

He yelled back, "Hi ladies. Ok, baby. Don't be too long. The pain is starting to come back. I might need another dose of pain medication."

We all frowned and went outside. We walked to Kim's car and I looked at my friends with tears in my eyes, "Girls, I just don't know how to get out of this. I really want out, but he makes me feel so damn guilty about trying to kill himself over me. I just don't know how to get out of this hell I'm in."

Amber got mad, "Fuck this shit! When his mama gets back, drop his ass off and tell him see ya."

Kim put her hand on Amber's shoulder, "Be quiet Amber. It's not that simple or easy. Lisa you can't let him keep you in this hell. He is working you right now. When do you take him back to his mother's?"

"She'll be home Monday night and I'm supposed to have him back at 8pm."

"Okay, don't say anything to him about not staying together. Just be cool the rest of this weekend and get him back to his mother's house. It's time you and I had a heart to heart talk, Lisa. Come over after you drop him off. We'll make it through this," Kim commanded.

I let out a few tears as we embraced each other. Amber's tone had softened up, "Lisa, I'm sorry for yelling earlier. But that damn Ron makes me so mad. He is a user and always has been. Playing on your emotions is wrong, but I guess I can't expect anything less from him. I love you, Lisa. Do us a favor, please call us and let us know how you are. Don't make us worry like that."

I looked at both of my friends, and knew they had my best interest at heart. I promised them I would call and not make them worry about Simone and I like that anymore. They got in the car to go, and I wished so badly I was going with them.

I went back into the house and checked on Ron.

"What did they want?" he asked with a nasty attitude.

"They were concerned about Simone and me. They came by to make sure we were alright."

"Yeah, I bet, they probably trying to figure out how to break us apart. Them your friends, but they some snakes. They just want you to be away from me so you can hang out with them." With a look of anger in his eyes, he demanded my attention. "Look at me Lisa."

I looked into eyes filled with hatred and rage, "They will not break us up again, Lisa. We are meant to be together. I will not stand for them or you jeopardizing us again. Mark my words, either we will live as a family or we won't live at all."

Damn! This is crazy. He is crazy. I looked at him for a moment trying to find the man that I'd fallen in love with years before. He was no longer there. I turned and walked towards the bedroom door. Before exiting the room a wave of anger came over me.

I turned around to this evil, s.o.b and said, "First of all, WE are not back TOGETHER. Second, if you think you are going to bully me into anything, you got another thing coming. I'm sick of you, and I'm sick of your shit. Mark my words Ron Sims, if you think I am going to sit back and listen to you threaten my child's life and put us both in danger, guess what? You won't have to worry about taking me out, because I bet I take care of you first."

I walked away infused with anger. He can't even move well and needs help getting to the toilet, and he's threatening me. The thing that made me the maddest was him threatening our daughter's life…his own flesh and blood. After this weekend, he is out of here and it is over. I'll be downtown Tuesday afternoon to file for a restraining order, and this time I am not lifting it. It's time to close this chapter of my life.

I went into my baby's room to check on her.

She grabbed me and held me so tight, "I love you Mommy."

I kissed her forehead, "I love you too, baby."

She looked at me for a moment with a sad look on her face, and in the lowest whisper said, "Mommy, I don't want Daddy to stay with us. When is he going home?"

That really surprised me.

"Real soon, baby…real soon."

Chapter 6

STACY

I've been spending more time with Mike since he said all of those wonderful things to me Labor Day weekend. I still haven't cut Mitch off, but I'm not seeing him as much as I was. I'm still undecided about whether I want to be in a 'real' relationship or not.

One thing I am sure about is I love holiday shopping and with Christmas less than a month away, I have to finish up. I don't want to be the one on the news on Christmas Eve. I finally finished and was waiting for my car at the valet.

I'm excited because Mike and I are supposed to spend Christmas together at his parent's house. Last year, Mitch was with his family and I was at home by myself. Even my mother was gone over her boyfriend's house. I bought a bottle of Moet and watched movies all day and night. I remember watching "Waiting to Exhale" and crying when Whitney Houston was listening to her married man talk to his wife on the phone.

I said I was done with Mitch after Christmas last year. In his usual fashion, he picked me up the day after Christmas. We went to the Antheneum Hotel and he fucked me like he missed me. I fell right back in, not to mention he gave me three grand as a belated Christmas gift.

Since I haven't been spending as much time with Mitch, he hasn't been giving up the money like usual. I can't lie, I miss it. I mean Mike is good to me, but he can't give me what Mitch can.

Finally they brought me my car. I've been to all my favorite stores; Saks, Neiman Marcus, and Macy's. The valet helped me put all my bags in the trunk, and I gave him a nice tip.

I was on my way down I-75, heading home when Mitch called.

"Hey baby, how you been?" he said when I answered.

I couldn't help it, I was glad he called. "I'm fine Boo. What you up to?"

"I was wondering if you had time for an old man like me."

I laughed at his little smart comment, "Why wouldn't I?"

"I've been hearing about you and Mike getting closer."

He was waiting for me to elaborate, but I didn't. He pushed a little harder, "Yeah, the word is you two may be getting married."

It felt kind of good to think Mitch may be a little jealous.

"Mitch, are you jealous or something?"

"Nah baby, it ain't nothing like that. I'm just used to you being all mine."

"Mitch, you were always the main one telling me you thought I should date other people. It's not like you didn't know I dated."

"You right baby, but I hope he can take care of you as good as I can."

He was starting to piss me off, "You know Christmas is coming up in a couple of weeks. Are you coming to see me this year on Christmas?"

"Now you know I can't do that Stacy. I'll call you. But you know on the holidays, I'm staying at home."

"Yeah, I know...well, you coming to get me or am I meeting you at the hotel?"

"Damn, baby I hope you don't think that's all I called for. I wanted to take you out to dinner. I'll be by to pick you up in an hour."

"Okay, see you then."

I got home and put my bags up, showered and changed. My mom was watching Cops. She was addicted to reality shows.

"Where you going, Ms. Stacy?"

"Mitch is picking me up, Mom."

"Stacy, you really need to leave his old ass alone. You got a good man in Mike. Don't fuck it up for a married man."

I smacked my lips, "I know Mom. I haven't committed to Mike yet."

She looked at me and patted the space next to her on the sofa, "Come here girl."

She turned the television off and asked me to sit down.

"Stacy, I know you love Mitch. Normally I don't bother you about who you date, but don't spend your whole life with a married man. Mitch is cool, but he isn't anything stable for you. I dated married men before, remember Harold?"

I thought back to Harold and remembered him coming over to the house. I answered, "Yeah, Mom."

"Well, Harold and I were dating for six years. That's right, six long grueling years of broken promises to leave his wife. Baby, during that time I went through several abortions that I never mentioned to anybody. All wasted time baby.

Once I made up my own mind to leave, most of the eligible, single men had already passed me by. I don't want to see that happen to you Stacy. Mike loves you, and Mitch lusts you. As you get older, you'll see love is lasting and lust is only for the time being."

I had to look at my mother. It's not often that we have a mother/daughter heart to heart talk. I always know that when she talks to me like that, she's really concerned. I told her that I loved her. Our talk was interrupted when I heard Mitch's horn blow. I got up to head for the door.

She called out to me, "Stacy...I love you too. Remember what I said and be careful."

Mike was out of town to see his grandmother in Chicago this weekend, so I didn't have to worry about telling any lies to him about my whereabouts. As I walked toward his car, I stared at Mitch wondering if this would be the last time we would really be together. I'm so confused.

KIM

It's cold out here. A Michigan winter can be something else. Lisa has been staying here with Malcolm and me since the end of September. That damn Ron has been harassing the mess out of her. She has a restraining order on him, but he has her too afraid to be in her own home.

After we sat down and had a heart to heart talk, I told her she was welcome to stay at my house whenever she needed a getaway. I finally told her about my past with Malcolm's father.

Malcolm's Dad was a piece of work. After he started at the plant, he developed a drug addiction that put my son and me in a bad situation. The job sent him for treatment and counseling, but he began to love being on medical and spending his whole check on his habit. Now Ron doesn't do cocaine, but alcohol and marijuana is still a habit.

Anyways, Joseph got so bad he was taking stuff out the house to sell. He even sold Malcolm's stroller. I see so many similarities in my life and Lisa's. Joseph did all the things Ron is doing now. He didn't shoot himself, but he did slice his wrist.

I started working four hours a day instead of a full eight hour shift, and ended up getting fired after three months for excessive absence, due to him acting a fool. Once he sliced his wrist and went to the hospital, he went on his best behavior and got out of the psychiatric ward. After that, it was like living in hell.

I had to watch him day and night, making sure he didn't do anything to Malcolm or me. He started with the threats of what he was going to do. I should have reported it to the police, but I didn't.

Finally, one night I was laying in the bed sleep. Malcolm was in his room. I woke up to being stabbed over and over again. I was sleeping with my money on me and he wanted it. I was planning to leave his ass, and he'd found out.

I had already secured an apartment here in Michigan and they called the house while I was sleeping to ask a few more questions. It was after office hours, and I couldn't understand why they would be calling so late. But I guess it wasn't their fault, they didn't know I was trying to leave my abusive boyfriend. The neighbor next door heard me screaming and called 911.

That's how I met Ms. Mary. She was the neighbor's sister. She and I would talk just about every day and she helped me to find an apartment in Michigan.

Joseph had managed to get out of the apartment before the police came, and took all my money. Ms. Mary kept Malcolm for me until I was out of the hospital. She brought him here to Michigan with her while I recuperated. I ended up staying with a friend I met while working for the telemarketing agency.

Joseph was finally caught and convicted. He served only nine years for the attack. I don't know where he is now. It's scary at times, because he could try and find me. I ended up working with the police and FBI to change my name and Malcolm's.

I left my friend Kelly's house, took a taxi ride to Midway Airport and left my past behind me when I moved here to Michigan. Lucky for me Malcolm was young enough to get used to his new name and I wanted to forget so bad, it wasn't hard to change from who I was to Kim McDonald.

I really don't like thinking back on all that, but once Lisa told me how Ron had threatened to kill her and Simone, I knew I had to.

When I made my journey from Chicago to Michigan, it was hard for me. My father and mother died when I was eighteen. They were the only children in both of their families, leaving me with no other family members to help me. But my parents did leave me something; a trust fund that I never told Joseph about.

When my mother was diagnosed with cancer, she made sure she made preparations for me. She lived with breast cancer for five years. The doctors only gave her two years, but she always told me she would make it to see me graduate from high school.

She made it, but by that Christmas, she was in hospice. She died before the New Year came in and never got to see her grand child I was pregnant with. It always makes me cry thinking about her, and wishing she could have seen Malcolm.

Lisa has taken Simone and Malcolm to Jeeper's. Simone really loves that place and even though Malcolm is a teenager, he loves watching Simone enjoy herself.

I'm home alone sitting on my chaise lounge with a glass of my favorite wine. I find myself staring out of my window, watching the snow fall and thinking how beautiful God has made nature.

I guess having company around the house isn't so bad, but I do love my alone time. I was sitting there daydreaming and the personal trainer entered my thoughts. After two glasses of wine I built up the nerve and I decided to call. I dialed his number from my cell phone, because I wasn't ready for any man to be calling my home.

He answered, "Hello?"

"Hello, may I speak with Alan Williams?"

"This is Alan, who am I speaking with?"

"Hi, Alan, you probably don't remember me, but you met me at the gym…"

Before I could finish my speech, he chimed in, "Oh, hey, how are you? I thought you weren't going to call me. I am so glad you called."

I couldn't believe his reaction, and thought, he must have me mixed up with somebody else. I couldn't help but ask, "Are you sure you know who this is?"

He laughed, "Yes, I'm sure. You had on a pair of black sweatpants and a white T-shirt that said 'On A Mission'. White New Balance gym shoes, and you were carrying a black and white New Balance gym bag."

I was impressed. I stumbled over my words, "Yes, that's me."

"I am so glad to hear your voice. I have a confession to make. I already know your name, because I asked the front desk. I've been eyeing you since I started at the gym."

I was flattered but let my insecurities show by saying, "I'm shocked you're interested in me."

"Why would you say that? You're beautiful."

"Maybe in a plus size way," I laughed.

His next comment made me feel comfortable about my size. He said, "Every woman wasn't meant to be small, and besides, every man doesn't like small women." He quickly asked, "So, when will I have the pleasure of taking you out?"

I had to be honest, "I haven't dated in a very long time. I'm not comfortable with any one coming to my home, so maybe we can meet for lunch."

"Lunch would be perfect, how about this Saturday at Andiamo's in Royal Oak?"

"That sounds perfect. How about 1 p.m.?"

"That's a good time for me."

"Well, I guess I'll see you at 1 p.m. on Saturday."

"I can't wait."

"Okay see you then…goodbye Alan."

I was testing the waters to see if he really knew my name. He laughed, "Goodbye Kim McDonald."

I hung up the phone, surprised at the fact that I actually called him, and now we are going on a date! Dayum! Things are finally swinging my way for a change.

AMBER

Ameri and I have been dating for six months now. I can definitely see us being together. He's been having a lot of problems with his soon to be ex-wife, but we are working through everything. Since he doesn't want her to bring up the fact that he is dating, generally we meet over my house. I have been over to his apartment in Livonia, but I don't go over there too often.

His brother, Shawn, is just as fine as he is, just a couple of years younger. I wish I could get one of my girls on him, but Ameri keeps telling me Shawn is in a committed relationship.

I did a little shopping after work and now I'm on my way home. I love shopping around the holidays. The sales are wonderful and the atmosphere around the malls is even better.

Now, I can't afford to shop at Somerset Mall like my girl Stacy, but Oakland Mall is just as good for me.

Once I get home, I'm going to see if my Boo is coming through. I call Ameri "My Boo" now. I haven't seen him in the last couple of days and I miss him.

He's been putting in some O.T. to get his son's Christmas all together. He loves those boys. After he's worked twelve hours and spent time with the kids, he ain't even been feeling like sex too much. I'm hoping if he comes over tonight, I can get a little somethin'…somethin'. I mean, once you get some good loving, you want it all the time.

I did over spend today. I bought gifts for Stacy, Lisa, Kim, and Simone. Also, I bought a couple of gifts for my co-workers in my department. Trying to get all these bags in the house is crazy. Finally after getting everything in, I rushed to see if my 'boo' had called me. No new messages. Well, let me try him again. I called him when I got off work earlier today, but he hasn't called me back. I hate when he doesn't return my phone calls.

What I thought I Wanted

Lately, he's been mentioning to me how crazy his soon to be ex-wife is. Hearing that makes me nervous, I don't want to have to cut a bitch! I remember one time, he told me she tried to run him over with her car because she had propositioned him and he declined her offer when they met up to get the kids. Another time, she told him he couldn't pick them up because he hadn't been fucking her lately, so she knows he's fucking somebody. Poor girl, I can only imagine how she feels, because Ameri is a good man. Oh well, consider that a lesson learned; if you want to keep your man, you gotta take care of home.

I called his cell phone and the voice mail picked up. I left another message, "Hey Boo, it's your baby. I've called you twice today and you haven't returned my phone calls. I hope everything is alright. I miss you. Call me."

After I hung up, I put all my bags up and decided to go out to Blockbuster Video to rent some movies. Soon as I got in the car, my cell phone started ringing. I knew it was him because I got the ringtone, "You, Me and He" by Mtume programmed for his cell phone.

I was excited, "Hey Boo!"

"Hey baby, sorry I didn't call you earlier. I was so tired when I got off work. I came in and went straight to sleep. What you doing?"

"About to go to Blockbuster and rent some movies, why?"

"I was hoping I could come by and see you."

"You know you can always come by, what time?"

"I'm on I-94 now, I should be there in about 20 minutes."

"Okay, I'll be home, see you in a few."

"See ya."

I was happy as hell! I ran in Blockbuster so fast and got back home in record time! I raced in the house, showered and put on some sexy pajamas. Now the only thing left to do was to wait for my man to arrive.

My phone started ringing, so I jumped up to answer it, "Hello…hello…hello." I hung up.

Again the phone rang, "Hello"

"Hey girl, it's Kim. What you doing?"

"Waiting on my man to get over here. Did you just call me?"

"I tried to call you, but the line was busy. I hung up and called back. Guess what Amber?"

Now this was unlike Kim, she never played the "Guess what" game. I played along, "What?"

"I got a date!!"

"Hell nah, Kim! You got a date? With who?"

She was so happy, "With the personal trainer at the gym."

"Damn! A personal trainer? Is he fine?"

"Amber, girl he is! I almost broke my neck on the treadmill when he smiled at me."

"When ya'll going out?"

"This weekend, we're meeting for lunch. Can you help me find something to wear?"

"Girl, I'm honored you asked me and of course I will. Let's leave after work tomorrow and see what we can find."

"Thanks, Amber. Now do me a favor, don't say anything to Lisa. She got enough problems and please don't tell Stacy, I don't want to hear her rules for dating."

"You got my word Kim. I won't say a thing."

Just then, Ameri knocked on my door. "I got to go Kim, see you at work tomorrow."

"Okay, and Amber…thanks!"

"Anything for you Kim."

We hung up and I sprung to my feet to answer the door.

We must have hugged and kissed at the door for twenty minutes. He couldn't keep his hands off of me. We finally broke apart long enough for him to ask if he can take a shower. I gave him a towel and let him do his thang.

I turned on my flat screen in the bedroom, put in a porno, got a bottle of wine and two glasses and waited on him to get out the shower. He came out naked and dripping wet. Damn! He was sexy as hell.

He looked at the television and said, "Baby, that's what I love about you. You look good and you a freak."

I smiled, walked up to his naked ass and gave him a glass of wine. I grabbed his manhood and told him, "You are so wrong for keeping this away from me. How can you get me all in and then cut me off."

He smiled, "Baby, it's only been a week."

I looked him in his eyes with a smirk on my face, "A week is too long."

He smirked back, "Well, I'm going to take care of you now."

We walked over to my King size bed and put our glasses on the nightstand. Quickly thereafter, we began our own symphony. He told me he likes pornos, which is a plus, because I love 'em! I love hearing another woman getting it good while I'm getting it good too.

Everything was going great until his cell phone started ringing. We ignored it the first five times, but it kept going off. He got up and looked at it. I could tell by the way he smacked his lips, it was 'her'.

He tied a towel around his waist and went out into the hallway, shutting the door. I could hear him yelling, "What is the problem? Well, that's too bad, you take care of it. I got to go."

I heard him hang up the phone and then he came back into my room. By the look on his face I knew the mood was blown.

"Boo, what's wrong?"

"She gets on my damn nerves. She acts like she can't do nothing without me."

"Maybe she knows she losing you and she can't stand it," I tried to rationalize.

"Yeah, but this is some bull shit."

"Come over here and let me make you forget about that nasty phone call."

He reluctantly walked over to me, and I let my mouth do the work. Before long, he was moaning and groaning and calling my name.

"Damn Amber, you do that shit soo good!"

I looked up at him and stopped long enough to tell him, "I know baby, that's cause I'm diggin' you."

We made love and after it was over, he told me he had to go. She wanted him to pick up the kids for the night. He said if he didn't, she wouldn't let him see them when he wanted to. I understood, but I hated to see him leave.

After he left, a sense of emptiness came over me. I'd gotten the sex I wanted, but the affection I needed after sex wasn't happening. After all that good lovin', it wasn't worth it.

I turned on the radio and listened to mix 92.3 fm. Ironically enough, Luther Vandross was playing "If only for one night." As I lay alone in my bed, I began to sing along with the words. I began to feel so sad for myself. I hoped the night would hurry by and tomorrow would be here, so I wouldn't have to suffer the loneliness I was feeling right now.

LISA

We had so much fun at Jeepers. Simone had a really good time. Malcolm pretended to be assisting Simone in some of the games, but I could tell he was enjoying himself as well.

"Okay Malcolm and Simone, what are we taking home for dinner?"

Simone was quick with her response, "Taco Bell."

73

Malcolm laughed and followed suit, "I can deal with Taco Bell."

Taco Bell it was. I drove down Eight mile road to the Taco Bell near Telegraph and placed our order. Malcolm has truly grown in the last couple of years. His stomach must be a bottomless pit, because he seems to never get enough food.

On our way back to Kim's house, I was so happy. I haven't had peace of mind like this in a long time. I heard my cell phone ringing in my purse and asked Malcolm to hand it to me. I knew who it was. I swear Ron must have a Lo-jack system on me that knows when I'm feeling good, because he always seems to call to mess it up.

"So where you at?" He started straight into his evil ass ways.

"Why you asking me where I am?"

He sounded pissed off, "I'm standing in front of the house. I've been ringing the bell for an hour and waiting on you. Where you at Lisa?"

"Look Ron, I'm not at home as you can see, and I won't be home any time soon."

"Oh, so you out hoeing around with my baby? Yo' dyke ass with some dude or some bitch?"

He knows how to hurt my feelings. I know I dress a little tomboyish, but that's just me. To try and get a rise out of me, he always results to calling me a dyke.

"Let me speak to my daughter, bitch!"

I looked in the rearview mirror at Simone, and pulled over. I turned around to the back seat and looked at her.

"Simone, your Daddy is on the phone. He wants to talk to you." I whispered to her, "Don't tell him where we are staying at, okay?"

She nodded her head. I gave her the cell phone.

"Hi, Daddy!" I knew he was asking her a million questions. Finally, she said, "Here mommy, I don't want to talk anymore."

I took the phone from her and got back on the phone "Hello?"

"Oh, so now you turning my daughter against me?"

"Why do you say that, Ron?"

"Shit, she don't want to answer no questions and don't want to see her daddy. I asked her did she want to spend some time with her daddy, and she said that she just wanted to be with you. What kind of shit are you telling her, Lisa?"

"Look Ron, I'm not telling Simone anything. Are you going to get her something for Christmas?"

"You know I ain't working and my medical checks aren't much, besides she don't want to see me anyway."

Just like Ron, always making excuses. He started getting more and more frustrated, "Look Lisa, I got a ride over here expecting yo hoe ass to be home, but you in the street with my fucking daughter. Bitch, I done told you, I ain't for that bullshit you keep putting out."

"I'm calling your doctor tomorrow and notifying the courts of your constant harassment. You keep on, and you're going to get locked up."

"Yeah well, if I do, I bet I take care of your hoe ass first. You and that little bitch I made."

Ron sure knows how to piss me off, but I didn't let it show to Simone or Malcolm.

"Well, Ron, I got to go."

I hung up the phone and was almost to Kim's house. I felt so good I didn't have to put up with his ass knocking on the door all night, hollering my name. I looked in my rearview mirror at my precious angel.

I figured I better get some protection for her and me. My local was offering a CCW class, and after hearing all the threats

What I thought I Wanted

Ron was making, I decided to enroll on Monday. I'm going to be ready for his ass. I thought about the story Kim told me about her ex and decided it won't be me running, it'll be his ass!

    A few minutes later, my cell phone rang again. It was Ron's mother. I let out a sigh and thought to myself, "Here we go."

    I answered on the third ring, "Hi Ms. Gladys. How are you?"

    She sounded in a panic, "Baby, I'm alright. Ron just called me. He is at your house in the cold. Where you at?"

    Since his suicide attempt, every time I don't do what he wants me to do, he tells his mama.

    "Where I am is not important. How can I help you Ms. Gladys?"

    "Baby, you know Ron. He got his friend Scooter to take him to your house. I tried to get him not to go, but he hadn't heard from you and went to check on you and the baby. Why you doing him like this, Lisa? You know what state of mind he in."

    We had pulled into Kim's drive way and I let the garage up and parked inside. I told Ms. Gladys to hold on while I got Simone out the car and motioned for Malcolm to take her in the house. I took the phone off of mute, "Ms. Gladys, are you still there?"

    "Yes, baby. I can't take much more of this. Why won't ya'll work this out? Ya'll promised to try when he was in the hospital."

    I cut her off before she could say another word, "Look Ms. Gladys, no disrespect, but your son has threatened my life and your grandchild's. I'm not going to stick around and wait to see if he makes good with his threats. And for the record, I didn't commit to being with Ron. You assumed I would work it out with him. I'm tired of Ron calling me a dike and my child a bitch. I'm not going to stand for that anymore. I'm telling you, so you won't have to guess, there is no Ron and me. I'm not getting back together with him and he will not see Simone."

Ms. Gladys began to cry. "Baby, please…think about what you doing to him. He told me about how you like women and don't want no man, but can't ya'll work it out?"

I couldn't believe what she just said.

She kept on talking, "Being funny like that ain't the worst thing in the world. Maybe ya'll could come to some type of agreement."

I had heard enough, she was just as crazy as he was.

"Look Ms. Gladys, that's your son, and I know you love him. But I can't be with Ron, he is physically and emotionally abusive. I can't have that around my baby."

She kept trying to convince me otherwise. Before hanging up, I spoke as sternly as I could.

"Ms. Gladys, I'm sorry you feel the way you do. I feel sorry for you, because Ron will be the death of you, not me or my daughter."

"Baby, he out in the cold…"

"Well, I suggest you get off the phone with me and call him back. Tell him he may as well come back home to you. I'm won't be back home tonight, so staying in front of my house will do him no good."

"But baby…"

I hung up without listening to another word.

I was so cold when I finally came into the house. Simone and Malcolm were sitting at the kitchen table eating and Kim was making a batch of purple passion. Just what the doctor ordered.

I went to my room and she followed close behind.

"Are you alright? Malcolm told me you were talking to Ron."

"Yeah, Kim I'm okay."

77

I told her he was at my house and how he called me all types of names. She shook her head.

"Kim, he always calls me a dyke. I know how I dress, but that shit makes me mad."

Kim looked at me, "Girl, you can't let that upset you."

"I know, but he used to say that in front of Simone all the time. She started asking me what a dyke was. I don't want her to ever think badly of me."

"She won't Lisa. She knows who loves and takes care of her. That's all that matters."

I took a long sip of my purple passion and felt at ease. I knew Kim was right, I just needed some reassurance. I went back into the kitchen, where my baby was, looking all sleepy. I picked her up and told her it was time for bed.

By the time I bathed her and got her in the bed, it was going on 11pm. I sat down in the family room with Kim and watched the news. The night was nearly over and I decided after talking to that asshole tonight, I'm putting my mother's house up for sale. I didn't want to let it go because it was the last thing I had that reminded me of her, but I knew even she wouldn't want me to be there under these conditions. First thing tomorrow morning, I'm calling a real estate agent and putting my past on the market. I owned that house free and clear, so going to a house note or rent would be an adjustment, but at least I would have peace of mind.

Chapter 7

KIM

It's Saturday morning and I'm nervous as hell. In less than three hours, I'm meeting Alan for lunch. Thanks to Amber, I got the perfect outfit and my hair and my nails are done.

After Lisa went to put Simone to bed the other night, Malcolm sat down and asked me the question I hoped would never come up. I was sitting in the family room and he came in and sat down next to me on the sofa.

He held my hand and asked, "Mom, what happened to my dad?"

I knew one day it would come and I had rehearsed it over and over again in my head how I would discuss it.

I took a deep breath, "Malcolm, I really don't know where your dad is. Do you remember him?"

He thought for a moment, "Vaguely…I remember him taking me to the park and sliding me down the slide."

"Well, I guess that's a good memory."

My son was mature and fifteen years old now. I knew he could handle the truth.

I asked him, "Have you ever noticed the scars on my legs and arms?"

"Yeah Mom, you told me you fell through a window when you were a little girl."

I felt bad I had lied to my son, but before I thought he was too young to understand. I grasped his hand tighter, "Honey, you know mama would never want to hurt you, right?"

"Yeah mama, I know."

"Well, I wasn't honest with you and lied to you for your own protection as a child."

He was paying close attention and hanging on my every word.

"Malcolm, these scars didn't come from falling through a window, they came from your father. He tried to stab me to death while I was sleeping. I have more scars on my chest and stomach. Your father was on drugs and I had made plans to relocate to Michigan. He found out and tried to kill me. That's how I met Ms. Mary. She was visiting her sister who lived next door to our apartment. Her sister called 911 and that's what saved my life."

His eyes were filled with anger and tears, "So my dad is out here somewhere?"

"Yes, he is. I don't know where and I don't want to know where."

"I hate him for what he did to you mama. Do you think he'll try to track us down?"

I exhaled a deep breath and looked at my son, "I don't know if he will ever find us. Have you ever heard of witness protection?"

"Yes Mom."

"Malcolm, I changed your name and mine for our own safety. We got new names and birth certificates. Yup, we have everything we needed to start over."

"So my name wasn't Malcolm, it was something else."

"Yes baby it was."

He leaned over and kissed me on the cheek and hugged me so tight.

"Mom, I'm glad you told me the truth. I appreciate you so much for what you sacrificed to protect me. I love you so much. Don't worry mom, this is between you and me. I'm just glad I know. I'm tired, so I'm going to turn in for the night. Good night."

I was so glad the conversation went like it did. Lisa had to think I was crazy. It appeared that I was watching the news, but I was so caught up in the conversation I just had with my son, that the television could've been watching me. She seemed to be a little preoccupied last night too, so we sat in silence pretending to watch the 11 o'clock news.

It's noon and time for me to head out. I checked my make-up and my hair. I went to the bathroom two more times before finally leaving the house. I stopped at the car wash to get some of the snow and ice off my car.

The ride to Andiamo's took less time than normal. I parked my car and headed for the door. I got there about 12:45. To my surprise, Alan was already there. He greeted me at the door and I followed him back to our table.

He looked good. He had on all black. Wool black pants, and a cashmere turtle neck that seemed to hug his muscular physique. He was such a masterpiece.

He helped me out of my coat and pulled my chair out like a gentleman. The waitress came and I ordered a glass of Chardonnay. He ordered a glass of White Zinfandel. He kept smiling at me until finally I said, "What?"

He smiled even harder, "I can't believe you called and we are here."

He can't believe that, and I can't believe he likes me. I wanted him to come clean. What is his angle? I knew he wouldn't tell me straight out, but I'm way past grown and don't have time to play games.

I asked, "Look Alan, what's the deal? You are an attractive man, who could probably have any woman you want. I'm having a hard time with this whole thing. Just come clean with me."

His face changed, "You want me to come clean?"

"Yes, I want you to come clean."

"Okay, here it goes. I have liked you since I first saw you, but was too afraid to say anything. I've been trying to get your attention for weeks. I like what I see. You come to the gym to work out, not to socialize or try to meet someone. I like that. You seem like you have your head on straight, and I like that. I

don't want an air head or someone who just wants to be pretty
and nothing else. I want the whole package, and you seem to be
it. I love thick, sexy women, and you represent them well. I don't
like thin women. I'm looking for a one on one relationship and I
am truly interested in you. Anything else you want me to come
clean with?

I was shocked, "No, I guess that sums it up."

We enjoyed our lunch and talked about our lives. I told
him about Malcolm. He told me he doesn't have any children.
After he told me his feelings, I let my guard down a little and had
a good time for a change. We sat a little while longer after the
waitress cleared our plates. I didn't want to leave his company.
He asked if he could see me again.

"Sure. When do you want to see me again?"

Without hesitation he said, "Later on tonight for dinner."

I was at a loss for words. I repeated him, "Later-on-for-
dinner?"

"That's what I said. Look Kim, I've been waiting for this
opportunity and I've enjoyed talking to you just like I knew I
would. I could wait for a week, but why when I know I want to
see you again tonight. You don't want to play games and neither
do I."

I agreed. "Tonight it is."

He smiled and leaned back in his chair, "Good, now
where should I take you tonight? Or will you come over to my
place so I can cook for you?"

"I feel good about you Alan. I'll come over to your place.
You bragged at how good you can cook, so let's see."

He helped me with my coat and we headed toward the
door. He opened the door to the restaurant for me to walk out. I
loved that he was a gentleman.

While walking to my car, he grabbed my hand. I haven't
held hands in a long time, except if you count Malcolm. It felt
wonderful.

I got into my car and couldn't wait for our second date later on tonight at 9 pm. He got into his black Lincoln Navigator and we headed out the parking lot.

The anticipation of tonight was overwhelming. I couldn't wait to call Amber and tell her all this stuff. I haven't been this excited in a long time. I went home on cloud nine to figure out what I was putting on for round two. I hope Amber's home. I pulled my cell phone from my purse and dialed her number.

"Hello," she answered on the first ring.

"Hey girl, my date is over and wait til' I tell you how it went."

She screamed, "Give me play by play girl and don't leave nothing out!"

AMBER

I'm glad somebody is having some excitement in their lives. Kim deserves it. She hasn't had a man in years. That vibrator she talks about can only do so much. Don't get me wrong, Ameri is still the man of my dreams, but he's got baggage.

We don't spend as much time together as I would like. That "soon to be ex-wife" of his is always manipulating their situation. I mean, she still tries to get him to have sex with her in order for him to see the kids. Always trying to get him to come over their house because something is wrong with the toilet, the car, whatever she can think of. He gets so frustrated.

We can be in my bed getting it on, and here his cell phone goes ringing. It fucks the mood up completely. I'm really falling for him, so I'm trying to be understanding. But when is it too much understanding?

I called the only one of my girls that has dated plenty of married men, Stacy. She told me to be suspicious of that brother.

"Sounds like he is still messing with his wife," she told me in her attitude voice.

She kind of pissed me off by saying that but I knew it was only because she was probably right. Truthfully, I was worried that he might be.

Well, tonight I'm going to sit down and talk to his ass about me, him, and his wife. I got to ask some questions, because this relationship is getting harder and harder by the day.

Don't get me wrong, Ameri is a sweetheart. I love being with him. Our sex life is the bomb, and he knows how to treat a lady. In fact, we are supposed to go away together for a couple of days during the Christmas holiday. I can't wait for that.

Since he doesn't have much money, I've planned our little getaway out. I booked us a room at Sybaris in Illinois. The room is the bomb. It has a swimming pool inside the room. I'm going to love finally getting a chance to sleep in his arms. We haven't actually spent a whole night together.

Just as I was getting ready to get into the shower, my phone rang, "Hello."

"Hey baby. What you doing?"

"Getting ready for you."

I could tell he was smiling, "That sounds good baby. Listen, I'm running a little late. She was supposed to be back here by seven so I could leave, but she hasn't made it back yet."

My excitement quickly turned to disappointment. On Saturday's, he takes the boys to their basketball game and out to lunch. He told me she had something else to do Saturday, but assured him she would be back no later than five so he could leave. Here we go again...

I mustered up my most understanding tone, "I guess I'll see you later then."

He quickly told me "Okay, see you then."

We hung up and I continued to get myself together. I got out the shower and put my p.j.'s on. Got me a glass of white wine and sat on my sofa. After two glasses, I picked up the phone and called my girl Stacy.

"What up Stacy? Busy?"

"Nah girl. Just laying around."

I needed someone to talk to and since I had confided in Stacy about Ameri, I only felt comfortable talking to her.

"Stacy, he was supposed to be coming over and got held up by her ass again."

She smacked her lips, "Look Amber, that man is still married. Don't waste your time sitting around waiting on him. You're setting yourself up for some serious heartache. See, when I date married guys, I always got somebody else on the side. You are putting all your eggs in one basket."

I smacked my lips, "He can't be doing that much with her, because he is giving it to me on the regular."

She didn't hesitate with her answer, "Look Amber, don't fool yourself. How you know he ain't staying there every night? Or at least some nights?"

I was feeling mad and stupid all at the same time, but I had to say something.

"Stacy, I got to be honest with you. I don't know what to think. One night, I looked through his wallet and got his address. Maybe I'm afraid to find out what's going on."

I guess when she heard I had the address, she couldn't help but ask, "Have you ever been by their house?"

Now Stacy was the only girl I knew brave enough to go to a married man's house. I was curious to see where he lived. I just didn't have the nerve to do a 'drive by'.

I came clean with my girl, "I got his address, but I haven't driven by."

Stacy jumped in, "Well, what the fuck you waiting on? Girl, you better than me. I couldn't help but spy on his ass."

I started getting more curious, "What if he catches me driving by?"

She spoke like a pro, "First of all, you wouldn't go by in your car. Second, it would be late at night, and third, that's what your road dog is here for."

We laughed. She started in again, "Look girl, it's 1 o'clock in the morning and he still hasn't shown up. This would be the perfect night to go by there. I can be over your house in fifteen minutes. You wit it?"

After downing another glass of wine, I said, "I'm with it."

With that said, Stacy told me she was on her way and I ran into my room to put on some clothes.

STACY

My girl Amber is going through it. She's really feeling Ameri, but I'm starting to think he's full of shit. Since Mike and I aren't going out tonight and Mitch is at home with 'wifey', doing a drive by at Ameri's house was right up my alley. I got dressed in a flash and was out the door.

On my way, I thought about Mike and Mitch. With Mike, it's nice to have a man all to myself. Life is comfortable with Mike and passionate with Mitch. I don't know what I'm gonna do.

I pulled up at Amber's home, called her on the cell phone and waited for her to come out.

She got in and I asked her, "You ready Amber?"

She sounded a little reluctant, "Yeah."

I could tell she was nervous. I programmed the address in my navigation system and we were on our way. We were laughing and talking on the way there and I brought something to help ease her tension.

I reached into my purse, and told her, "Fire this up girl and calm your ass down."

87

Now we didn't smoke weed that often, usually when we're all together, but this was extenuating circumstances and my girl needed it. As we got closer to Westland my heart was racing. Listening to the navigation system tell us to exit off I-96 at Merriman Road, we both knew we were getting closer.

We stopped our normal chatting and concentrated on the sound of the voice telling us which way to go. As we turned on to his street, the navigation system said, "Your destination is ahead on the right."

I slowed down as I approached a nice brick ranch home with attached garage. The neighborhood was nice. As we crept past the house, she saw two vehicles in the driveway. His black Tahoe, which Amber knew by the rims and a black Explorer.

She turned to me, "He is still there. Maybe she just got in."

I know my girl is not a dummy. It's 3am and both cars are at home. I had to set her straight.

"Amber, I don't think she just got home."

She looked like she wanted to cry, "How do you know, Stacy?"

As I turned around at the end of the block to go back past the house, I pulled over and said, "Okay, you need evidence, hold on."

I parked and had already cut my lights out. I got out my car and ran toward Ameri's house. I always wore black when I did late night drive bys like this. I ran up to both trucks and touched the hoods. Both were cold. That's all I needed.

I got back to my car and told Amber, "Both trucks are cold, so they have been sitting for awhile."

As we drove off, she started to cry. I felt bad for her, but it's good she knows sooner than later. I wish I would have been smarter about Mitch and myself.

Mitch gave up the dollars, but we would never have a real relationship. He never lied and promised he would be with me, but I think I always hoped he would. Ameri is telling Amber he is about to divorce his wife and how they aren't getting along, but he's still at the house with her at 3 o'clock in the morning. I hope this is enough for Amber to move on. I don't want her caught up in the same web that I'm in.

We drove back to Amber's house in silence. She finally broke the silence, "Damn, Stacy. I am so hurt. I don't know what to do."

I was pissed, "Well, when his ass calls, see what he says. Don't let on you know anything, just see what he says."

She dried her eyes, "Stacy, I'm not like you. I have a hard time hiding my feelings."

I was stern, "Look Amber. Keep it together, stack your evidence and then hit him with it."

As we finally got to her home and walked through the door, her phone was ringing. She picked it up and I could tell it was him. After she hung up the phone, I asked, "Girl, what did he say?"

She sighed, "He said he fell asleep waiting on her and she didn't wake him up when she came in."

I could tell my friend believed that bullshit. I looked at Amber for a moment, then said, "Amber, I can't change how you feel about him, but you better be careful. I think Ameri is playing a dangerous game and I don't want to see anything happen to you. Just keep your eyes open and try thinking with your mind, not your heart."

I hugged my friend and was out the door. It was 5am and I was tired. As I was on my way back home, I thought about Mike and was actually glad I didn't have to go through that kind of shit with him. This made my relationship with Mitch seem even more meaningless. I guess going through this with Amber is helping me to see what is best for me.

Mike called me just before I got home, "What you doing out this time of the morning?"

I smiled at his concern, "I was out with Amber, trying to prove a point to her."

With concern, "Well, that's nice you are trying to prove a point to Amber, but you're my baby and I love you. I don't want you running around the streets all night. Okay?"

Now usually, I'm not receptive to any man checking me, but after reflecting on my relationships and looking at Amber's, I welcomed it.

With a smile in my heart and on my face, "You're right baby, I'm sorry. I just pulled into the driveway and am on my way into the house."

He spoke softly, "Okay baby, I'll see you tomorrow. I love you."

Mike has always shared his feelings with me. He never had a problem telling me he loves me. I just never say it back to him. I've never said it to any man. Just can't bring myself to do it. Tonight was an eye opener for me. I still don't know what I'm going to do about Mitch, but my feelings have truly grown for Mike.

I haven't even been seeing any of my other money men. I can't even believe that, and not getting that extra money isn't even bothering me. Actually, I have a 401K, mutual funds, and IRA's set up. I really don't need it. I just like getting money.

After my man said he loved me this morning, without hesitation I said those words back to him, "I love you, too." Without another word, we hung up.

E'nise

Chapter 8

LISA

I really didn't want another house and I didn't want an apartment for Simone. I wanted her to have plenty of room to run around. I have a great real estate agent. He finally found me a condo in Farmington Hills.

I never thought I would move out of my mother's home, and even more so, never thought I would move out of the city of Detroit. I really like the condo. I showed Kim, and she absolutely loved it. I mean, it will give me peace of mind from Ron. I know he isn't going to be coming by and knocking on the door at 3am. The Farmington Hills police don't play that shit.

It's been crazy. I've got a few people looking at my Mom's house. No one has made an offer yet. Once Ron saw the Century 21 sign go up in the yard, he had a fit. He called me everything, but a child of God. I'll be glad to close on my condo, so Simone and I can get back to somewhat of a normal life.

Don't get me wrong, Kim has been great. I think she needs her space. She's dating a little now, and she might want Alan to spend the night. She says she is not at that point yet, but I know she has got to be getting horny.

He came over to the house a couple of days ago, and that brother was fine as hell. I don't know what Kim is waiting for. He seemed to be a little put off by my appearance. I've always looked like a tomboy and some men think I'm a dyke by appearance.

When Alan first saw me, I can tell he thought Kim and I had something going on. I tried to make him feel at ease by saying how nice it was to finally meet him. I introduced him to Simone and she thought he was great. Simone usually doesn't take to people that easy, but she liked Alan.

It's been a while since I've been to my favorite after hour spot. Since the birth of Simone and trying to make my relationship work with Ron, I stopped going there.

Once Ron and I started having problems and we broke up, I started going back from time to time. That's my release these days.

It's been a while since I've had sex and my hormones are racing. I just need to get out and be in the company of others. I've always been a freak. I think that's why Ron has such a hard time letting go. I really love sex, but I've been trying to keep my sexual appetite under wraps since I had Simone.

So tonight, Kim is watching Simone and I told her I was going out to movie and then to the bar. I told her, I just needed to get out for a while. Truth is, my sexual appetite is killing me and I have got to scratch this itch.

I got to my spot about one and waltzed in. I went straight to the bar and ordered a shot of Patron with a Long Island Iced Tea to loosen up.

I was looking pretty damn good tonight. I've been told I have a body like a model. I wore a skirt and a see through blouse. I took my bra off before I got out the car.

The cold air outside made my nipples hard, so I knew I would be getting the attention I needed. See, my after hour spot wasn't just any after hour spot. It was for people like me.

After standing at the bar for a while, I downed my shot and started walking around with my Long Island Tea.

Some people wear a mask to hide their faces. As I walked through, I noticed it was some fine brothers in here. They were checking me out and I was checking them out, until I finally focused in on what I wanted.

I could tell by what I was seeing, my appetite was going to be fulfilled tonight. As we made eye contact, the gesture was made to go to the rooms up stairs. This spot had rooms you could hook up in. You pay a membership fee and must have a test to prove you are free from diseases and drugs. They even have their own doctor that you go and see for this club, to make sure you aren't changing the outcome of the test.

As we got upstairs to the room, we started kissing. It felt so good. Feeling those hands up my skirt, touching my ass was like heaven. We shut the bedroom door and locked it. As we managed to make it to the bed, I was wet as hell. Those hands caressing my breasts, I was sure I was going to come any second now, but I had to see what I was getting. I slowly unbuttoned the shirt and I couldn't help but rush to the pants.

After we were naked, I fell back on the bed as she tasted my wetness. A woman sure knows how to please another woman. She made me cum and I felt the pressure of the world escape from my body.

I flipped her over and returned the favor. I then went to my oversized purse and pulled out my strap on and lubricated it. She smiled and turned around with her ass in the air, waiting for me to fuck her. As I was fucking her, I came again. She was screaming and I couldn't stop. I could tell she was getting closer to her orgasm and I asked her, "Are you ready?"

She screamed, "Yes, yes, yes!"

I started fucking her harder until she finally came. Even though I love the fellas, every now and then, I get an urge for a woman.

After it was all over, we went into the bathroom attached to the bedroom and showered together. I was horny all over again. We went back to the bedroom and this time, she fucked me.

It was great and I was ready to resume my regular life. We both washed up and headed downstairs. We never really said any words to each other. As we approached the bottom step, we looked at each other and smiled, silently thanking one another.

I guess she was going through a lot too. Her face told me she needed me as much as I needed her.

Once back downstairs, I went to the bar and had one more shot for the road. I watched my mystery fling disappear into the crowd. It was 4am when I reached Kim's house. I changed clothes and lay in the bed. I was so tired. Before I finally drifted into a deep sleep, I wondered if hooking up with a woman occasionally made me gay?

KIM

It's Christmas Eve and Alan is decorating my Christmas tree with Malcolm. I was really surprised Malcolm took to Alan as quickly as he did. I talked to Malcolm about Alan before I ever introduced them. Malcolm told me he was glad I was dating and couldn't wait to meet Alan.

Malcolm looked at me and spoke like a grown man, "Mom, I know you have to get lonely sometimes. I'm getting older and understand that. You've been through a lot, and most of the things you've done were to protect me. I appreciate that, but I want you to be happy and to have a life. Soon, I'll be going to college and I don't want you to be alone. It took you a long time to meet someone, so I know he must be alright."

That conversation made me so proud of my son. He is truly turning into a decent young man and is nothing like his father.

It was nice to watch the two men in my life laughing and talking. It's been about a week since Lisa moved into her new condo. She is happy to have her own place.

I asked her to come over, but she insisted she wanted to spend Christmas Eve with her daughter in their new home. I guess that's understandable.

After my fellas finished the tree, we watched movies. I popped popcorn and it was a nice evening. After the first movie Malcolm retired to his bedroom.

"I'm going to bed. It's after midnight, Merry Christmas mom and Alan. I won't be up early tomorrow. See you when I wake up."

After Malcolm walked out of the room Alan went to the closest to get something out of his coat pocket. He came back and sat on the couch next to me.

He spoke softly, "Kim, I know we haven't been dating for long, but I'm really drawn to you."

He opened up a jewelry box, with a beautiful diamond charm bracelet in it. "Please, accept this gift."

It had beautiful diamond charms hanging from it. There was a dumbbell, a heart, a little boy with a blue stone, a lock and key, and a bell.

He explained the meaning behind each charm: the boy being Malcolm, the lock, key and heart, meaning key to unlock his heart, and the bell meaning wedding bells to come.

I was astounded. I hugged and kissed him. This was the best Christmas present ever. He told me Malcolm helped him pick it out. That made it even better. I went to my room and brought back to presents for him.

Alan opened the first gift. To his surprise, it was a chain with a diamond key charm hanging from it. He looked a little quizzical, and asked "What does this mean?"

I opened the top of my robe to reveal the diamond lock dangling from my chain.

I smiled at him and said, "I guess great minds think alike."

We kissed briefly before he opened his second gift. As he opened it he noticed the box said "Fredericks." He was really looking puzzled.

He opened it slowly then pulled out a garter belt, some thigh hi's, a bustier and a thong bikini; all in red.

He opened the card that lay beneath. It read, "Can't wait till you see me in this."

He smiled and we shared a passionate kiss.

"I can't wait either."

It was four in the morning, I asked him to stay over. We went to my room and I gave him a pair of pajamas I had bought for him. It was nice to sleep with a man that held me close and tight. We didn't have sex, but the compassion and warmth of those arms around me made me feel secure and safe, safer than I had felt in a long time. We fell asleep in each others arms and it was blissful.

We woke up the next morning and I called all my girls and wished them a Merry Christmas. Stacy was spending Christmas with Mike. Amber was waiting on Ameri to come over and Lisa was playing with Simone and her toys.

I made my guys brunch: eggs, sausage, waffles and hash browns. While I was cooking Malcolm opened his gifts. He got a brand new Dell Computer, clothes and cologne. Alan bought him a pair of Air Force Ones.

He went to his room lugging his computer and I could tell by the noise he was putting everything together. I can't remember the last time I had been so happy.

A year ago, I cried all Christmas Day because I was lonely. I prayed for God to send me what he wanted for me, and look at this Christmas. I didn't know God would send him in such a fine package. I mean, I know I'm his child and he loves us all, but he must really love me. I didn't think I was worthy of a man that looks like this. A man that treats me nice and isn't just trying to get some butt is all I ever wanted. But honestly, I can't wait for him to try!

Malcolm wanted to go over his friend's house, down the street. I had no problem with that. After he left, Alan asked if he could take a shower before he ate. I got him a towel and toothbrush. My room has a bathroom inside and while I was making up the bed, Alan began to undress. I almost fell over the bed looking at this fine specimen of a man. He had it going on in

97

every area. I was scared that since he was a built guy, he wouldn't have nothing going on in those pants. At least that's what I've always heard about body builders. Well, the next time I hear a woman say that, I will sure tell her, that ain't true!

He asked me to take a shower with him. He assured me, no sex, just passion. After looking at his body, I didn't want to take my clothes off.

I was hesitant, but I walked into the bathroom and started to undress. He skillfully aided me. Alan slid my pants down to my ankles then waited patiently for me to step out of them. On the way up to my shirt, he placed subtle kisses on my thighs. I shivered at every kiss. Then he lifted my shirt, and once again, waited for me to raise my arms. Alan was such a gentleman. He popped my bra as I nervously removed my boy shorts. He stepped back in awe. I was a bit confused, but welcomed the compliment anyways. We showered and held each other, and all I can say is "Thank you, God."

AMBER

Since that night Stacy took me by there, things just haven't been the same. I mean, I still care for him deeply, but my antennas are up. It seems like I can't get enough of driving by Ameri's house. I've been switching cars with my mother the last few times. I told her I needed more room to help Lisa move. That being far from the truth, Lisa has already moved and is in her new place enjoying life.

It's Christmas and he hasn't made it over here yet. He told me he would be by after his kids opened up their presents and had dinner with them. He didn't want this year to be hard for them, since it was the first year of him not living in the house together.

I figured he would be here by 8pm. It's now 9:30pm, and I haven't received even a phone call yet. How inconsiderate can he get?

I don't know why I keep letting this thing linger on. I really need to end it. When we're together, it's great, but it seems we're more apart than together. I really want to drive by there.

I transferred my home phone to my cell phone, in case he calls. Curiosity has me and I'm out of here. I jumped on I-96 headed to his house one more time.

Even the songs on the radio are irritating me. All the radios stations were playing the Temptations, Donny Hathaway, and any other artist that has ever made a Christmas song.

Ironically, I was coming up on Merriman road and Johnnie Taylor's "It's Cheaper to keep her" was playing on WJLB. I wonder is that how Ameri is thinking. Maybe this divorce thing is too much for him.

As I turned down his street, it was lit up with beautiful Christmas lights and decorations. I slowly approached his house. Thank God for the snow, it gave me an excuse to slow down. Their front window curtains were wide open and you could see the Christmas tree. I couldn't believe my eyes!

I thought I saw a man that looked like Ameri sitting in a chair and a woman sitting on his lap smiling and watching something. No, I couldn't have. I turned around and crept by slowly, again.

I didn't see anyone through the window this time, but the front door was open and I saw Ameri coming out. I was terrified. I just kept my head straight and pulled my hat further down on my head. I made it out of there and back on the freeway, heading home.

This was a miserable Christmas. I was alone and lonely. No present to open for me and no one to share the holiday with. I was too embarrassed to call anyone or go over anybody's house.

What I thought I Wanted

All I have to look forward to are the two days we are supposed to spend in at Sybaris in Illinois. I hope he doesn't let me down. I've spent money making reservations and everything. He finally called at midnight. "Hey, baby! You sleep?" I was pissed, not sleep.

"No, just upset that you didn't even call to say Merry Christmas."

He didn't even act like my madness fazed him, "Can I come through?"

Like the sucker I usually am, "Sure, Ameri, come on…it's only the day after Christmas."

I guess he really takes me for granted.

"Well, I'm on Jefferson already, so I'll see you in a minute."

I was glad he was coming over but I felt so stupid. This was the worst Christmas I'd ever had. I opened the door for him and he came in like nothing was wrong. He sat down, and pulled out a small box from his jacket pocket. He gave me the small jewelry box that held a beautiful pair of diamond hoop earrings. I was so happy he thought enough to by me a gift.

I couldn't wait to tell him my surprise. I had so much excitement in my voice, "Thank you for my gift baby. Well, you know how you said we were going to spend a couple of days together during this week…I've made all the reservations and, we are spending two nights at Sybaris in Illinois."

As I finished my speech, I gave him the brochure. I was so excited.

"One of my friends went there before, and she said it would be perfect for us. No interruptions and its really low key."

He didn't even crack a smile.

"What's wrong? You don't like it?"

He looked at me, "Baby, I wish you wouldn't have done this."

I got instantly mad, "Why, Ameri!?"

100

His voice began to crack, "I...I...I don't know if I can make this. I was supposed to keep my boys a couple of days this week."

By this time I was fuming, "Okay, well keep them Monday – Wednesday. We don't have to check in until Wednesday night and we'll be back on Friday."

He shook his head, "Damn! Amber, I wish you would have told me."

That was it, all I saw was red, "Yo' ass told me we were spending a couple of days together during the holiday, and this is the holiday. I told you I was going to plan something for us to spend sometime together. You agreed. As a matter of fact, you said, 'you can plan whatever and wherever.' You don't remember that?"

He stood up, "Yeah, I remember...but...look Amber, I'm sorry. I'll try and work this out. Can you get your money back?"

"Fuck you, Ameri! You've been bullshitting me from the start."

He grabbed me up from the sofa and hugged me, "Don't act like that."

He got to rubbing all over me, and feeling me up. That's how he always got out of our arguments.

"Not this time, Ameri. If you aren't at my house on Wednesday by 5pm, don't bother coming or calling again."

I walked to my front door and opened it. I looked him in his eyes as he stood watching me from the sofa, "Have a good time with your boys Monday, Tuesday and Wednesday. I WILL NOT talk to or see you until Wednesday at 5pm."

He put his coat back on and headed my way. He stopped briefly at the door to try and give me a kiss. I turned my head and said, "See you Wednesday."

He looked at me and walked out my front door. I slammed the door and sat on my sofa pissed. I can't believe his ass.

About twenty minutes after Ameri was gone, I was watching television. The phone rang, I knew it was him. I looked at the caller ID, and the call was blocked. He was probably thinking I wasn't going to answer, so he blocked his phone number.

I answered with an attitude, "Hello!"

I could tell someone was holding the phone.

"Hellooooo!"

Still no answer, he was pissing me off.

"Look, it's no need of you calling and not saying nothing. I know you're on the phone. I can hear you breathing. If you don't want to talk, stop calling me!"

I held the phone for another thirty seconds, still nothing.

"Well, don't call back until you're ready to talk."

I hung up. That was so stupid. He probably just wanted to see if I was up or if I was going to ask him to come back over. No chance of that happening. I am sticking to my word, if he doesn't show up on Wednesday, it's over.

STACY

Christmas Day has been wonderful. Mike came over and we are spending it with my mom and her boyfriend. I never dreamed Christmas could be so nice. Usually, I'm moping around the house, sad because Mitch can't be there with me or we can't be together.

After the first few years we were together, I got used to him not calling on the holidays. I pretty much knew the holidays were for his wife and family. Still my heart would ache. I couldn't understand how he just couldn't call me.

But this year is different. I have a man in my life that is here 100%. He took care of me for Christmas. I got a fur jacket, and some Gucci boots. He knows my style. I even bought him some Cartier glasses. I knew I was really feeling Mike, because I usually don't spend loot like that on a man.

We had been at my Moms most of the day, and he decided he wanted to go visit one of his Aunt's on his mother's side of the family. He told me he wanted me to go with him. I'm so used to a dude coming to get me and hit a hotel room, I didn't know how to act when he said he wanted me to meet his family.

I wasn't going to turn him down. I mean he knew my whole past and he even knew I still had feelings for Mitch, but he didn't let that stop him from loving me.

I don't know how long this thing with Mike is going to last, but I'm staying on this ride until I have to get off. We got into his Cadillac Escalade and headed to his Aunt's house. She stayed off 7 Mile Road like me, but closer to the Lodge Freeway. It was only about ten minutes from my house.

Mike is always a gentleman. He opens my car door every time. We were riding down 7 Mile, when my cell phone started ringing. I figured it was some more of my relatives calling to wish us a Merry Christmas. When I looked at the phone, I couldn't believe my eyes. It was Mitch.

Mike asked, "Who is that?"

I said, "Mitch."

He kept his eyes on the road and said, "Well, answer it Stacy."

I didn't know what to do. Was I going to disrespect Mike or Mitch?

I answered, "What's up?"

Mitch chimed right in, "Hey, how you doing?"

I was totally uncomfortable, "I'm fine."

"You always say I don't call on the holidays, so I just called you for a minute."

I was happy in a round about way, "Thank you. I'm out right now so I'll talk to you later."

I could tell Mitch was uneasy, "You out! You by yourself?"

Damn, he was putting me in an even more awkward position.

"No, I'm out with Mike."

I knew that would make Mike feel better that I acknowledged him.

"Out with Mike...on the holiday...I guess ya'll getting closer than I thought."

I just kept quiet.

"Damn! In a minute, you won't have time for an old man like me."

I didn't know what to say. I guess Mitch is a little jealous, because his next comment shocked me.

"Is he giving it to you like I do?"

I had to say something then, "Look Mitch, this isn't the time. I have to let you go."

I couldn't believe I said that, and I don't think Mitch could, "Look babe, I know you wit yo' boy toy and I got to go. Let's get together tomorrow. I got to give you your present and you got to give me mine."

I know he's talking about some pussy and it made me mad. Usually I am all in when Mitch wants to see me after the holiday. I knew I was going to get some money and some good dick. I surprised myself with the next comment.

"Mitch I don't know if that is possible, because Mike and I are going to be together tomorrow as well. I have to let you go, talk to you later."

I hung up before he could even make another comment. I felt good. Finally, I felt liberated! I turned down Mitch and raised Mike up. I could see the smile on Mike's face. I grabbed his hand and held it as we continued our ride toward his Aunt's house.

I had put my phone on silent so it wouldn't be ringing over his family's house. After a couple of hours, I excused myself to the bathroom. After doing my business and washing my hands, I reached into my purse to apply some lip gloss to my lips and looked at my phone. I had three messages. I checked the call log and all of them came from Mitch.

I couldn't believe he was calling that much on a holiday. I listened to the first message: *"Yeah, you think you something now that you wit yo boy. It's cool. I'll wait for you. I guess you've had to wait for me before. Just don't let him beat that pussy up too bad. I need my shot too."*

Damn, that hurt. Mitch ain't never said nothing like that before. He has always known I dated more than just him. As a matter of fact he encouraged it. He said 'so I wouldn't get too attached to him'. Now he's acting like an asshole.

I didn't even listen to the rest of the messages. If it were more like that one, I can do without that.

Mike and I finished up our visit and went back to his house. We took a shower and lay naked in his bed just holding each other.

Finally he said, "Good night, baby. I love you."

I quickly replied, "I love you too Mike."

He laid there for another few minutes before he said, "Baby, do you think you could ever love me like you love Mitch?"

I turned around to face him, and stared into his eyes, "What makes you think I love Mitch more than you?"

He smirked, "The way you talk to him. You are so careful in how you choose your words. Nobody else may see it, but I know you love him."

I looked even deeper into my Prince Charming's eyes, "Baby, I'm not going to lie to you. I do love Mitch. I love you as well, but the love I have for you is so different. I fell in love with the idea of Mitch but I'm falling in love with the realness of this relationship with you. I know I don't want to lose you for him. We are still growing Mike, let us continue to grow."

He kissed my forehead and said, "Thank you, baby. Good night for real this time."

I smiled at this wonderful man, "Good night."

E'nise

Chapter 9

<u>KIM</u>

I haven't been seeing a lot of my girls since Alan and I have been hanging out. It's nice having a man around the house. It's New Year's Eve and Alan and I are spending the night at the Westin Hotel, downtown.

I'm a little nervous. I haven't been with a man in years. I guess you can't count my large vibrator I keep wrapped in a towel.

Now Alan and I have been getting close to going all the way. He is now my trainer and helps me at the gym a lot. Boy, when he places his hand on my thigh or hip when we're working out together, it drives me crazy. Sometimes I mess up on the moves his teaching me just so he can touch me again.

I just got out of the shower and I'm getting ready for what could be the biggest night of my life. Let me call him and see what time he is coming to get me.

"Hello Alan, I'm sorry to bother you, but I just wanted to know what time are you coming to get me?"

In his sexiest voice he said, "I'll be there around 6pm. What are you doing?"

"Oh, I just got out the shower, why?"

He gave a small chuckle, "Are you naked?"

I started getting aroused just by his questions, "Yes I am."

"Umm, that sounds good baby. Why don't you lay back on the bed for me?"

I couldn't resist. I followed his directions and took my robe off and lied down. I asked in my most sensuous voice, "Now what you want me to do?"

He told me in his commanding voice, "I want you to open those legs and let me give you what you need."

I couldn't help but do it, "Damn! I love when you talk like that. Can I touch it?"

"Yeah baby. You know you can, but first I got to put this hard on inside of you."

I could almost feel him entering me. I moaned, "Ohhh Baby. That feels so good."

I was on my way. He told me to play with my clit and I did. I couldn't help but get into this, "Baby I want you to imagine my full lips all over your throbbing penis. Sucking and licking."

He started moaning, "Yeah, baby."

We both started moaning and I screamed, "Baby I'm cumming!"

He said, "Don't stop. Keep working that pussy."

Before I knew it, I heard him say "Ohhhh my God...Shit...Damn, baby!"

As he came, so did I and it was marvelous. We've been having phone sex a lot lately and it's the bomb! It's not the same as sex, but it helps relieve the pressure.

After we came down off our high, he told me he couldn't wait for tonight. We hung up and I pulled myself together and couldn't wait to feel a real man on top of me, in me. I am long overdue.

Alan was punctual as usual. Malcolm was staying over his best friend's house. Alan took my bag to his car and we were off to our night together. After arriving at the hotel, we ordered room service. Alan had brought some Moet and Jose Cuervo 1800 Silver. When I saw that, I knew we were in for a wild night.

He brought his DVD player and hooked it up to the television. We had a suite with a whirlpool tub. He must have gotten the room early, because there were rose petals all over the bed and in the bath water of the whirlpool tub.

As we started kissing, there was a knock on the door, "Room service." He opened the door and the attendant rolls in this cart of food.

Alan tipped the waiter and he was on his way. I walked over to the spread to find appetizers: Buffalo wings, and two salads. Alan knew I loved Buffalo wings.

He walked over to me and grabbed my ass. He whispered in my ear, "I don't want any reason for us to have to leave this room."

I smiled and he began to undress in front of me. I stood there watching. He walked over to me and began to undress me. After we stood in front of each other in our birthday suits, we got into the whirlpool. He turned on a porno and poured us a shot of tequila and a glass of Moet. I was feeling good. We soaked, talked and drank. It was wonderful.

After a while we got out and I went to the bed to lotion up. He came over and stood in front of me. Man, this guy was perfect.

A well oiled machine stood in front of me with a shaft that was at full attention. I put my lips on it. I hadn't had my lips wrapped around something this luscious in years and I wanted him to know I appreciated every inch of it.

He was getting close to climax, and he gently pulled this rock hard shaft out of my wet mouth and pushed me back on the bed. He licked and kissed every inch of my body. I was ready, ready to feel that penetration. He guided his hardness into me and it felt like heaven. I came within seconds.

We made love for what seemed like hours. I enjoyed every inch and minute of it. He was just my type, big enough to hurt me. Sex feels so good when you got a man with enough to feel you up and have a little overflow.

Our night was wonderful. We would rest and make love again. By midnight, he was fucking me. He was giving it to me hard and raw, he said, "Happy New Year, baby."

I was loving the raw fuck so much that between my screams I said, "Don't call me baby when you fucking me like this. Call me Bitch!"

He smiled and it seemed to have turned him on even more. He picked me up and wrapped my legs around him. Grabbing my ass and fucking me standing up, he said the words I was longing to hear, "Happy New Year, Bitch."

I smiled, "Thank you, Daddy...Happy New Year to you."

We fell asleep that night watching "You've Got Mail" with Meg Ryan and Tom Hanks. I love that movie. I love the love story. I was so happy and pleased with my life right now. Nothing seemed as if it could go wrong.

I checked on Malcolm and wished him a Happy New Year. I called home to check my messages. I know Lisa, Stacy, and Amber have probably called me. I didn't tell them I was spending the night with Alan. I listened to my messages and sure enough my girls called. I couldn't wait to tell them what I was doing. They were going to be so happy for me.

I called Lisa first, "Hey girl. What you doing?"

She was watching television and Simone was sleeping, "What you doing? You sound happy."

I laughed, "Oh, I'm spending the night with Alan."

"Hell naw, hell naw...hold on, I'm calling Amber."

She clicked over to put Amber on three-way. Lisa clicked back in.

I heard Amber's voice, "Hell naw. This bitch getting it on and we at home alone."

We all laughed. I told them, "It's about time. Don't ya'll think?"

They both said how happy they are for me. I was laughing with them when Alan came out of the bathroom. I looked at him smiling at me with that devilish grin.

"Look ladies. I have to go. My man needs me."

We all bust out laughing.

"Talk to you two later."

They both said, "Bye hot mama!"

After hanging up, Alan came over to me and put his arms around me.

"You make me so happy."

I was happier than ever. As I held him, I didn't want this night to end.

LISA

It's New Year's Eve and Ms. Mary is watching Simone for me. I was getting ready to get out for the night when Amber called me with Kim on the phone. I'm so glad my girl is finally getting some much needed "quality time" with a special someone.

My phone has been ringing off the hook. Somehow Ron had gotten my number. He's been doing his usual calling and harassing. Talking about how much he misses Simone and me. With the restraining order in place, I feel a little safer.

The phone is ringing again. I can't wait until Monday morning. I'm calling the phone company to change my number and making sure I remember to make it unlisted.

I looked at the caller ID, "anonymous caller." Soon as I answered the phone I heard, "I'm gettin' tired of yo' fuckin' games Lisa. I wanted my daughter today, so she can spend New Years Eve with me. You actin' like a bitch!"

It's funny, as you grow out of a relationship, the harsh language doesn't bother you as much.

I calmly replied "Look Ron, you know you are not even supposed to be calling me. You put yourself in this position when you threatened my life and your daughter's life. Now, I will bring Simone by your mother's house tomorrow afternoon for the hours specified by the court and you can see her."

He couldn't stand me being this calm, "Lisa this some bullshit. Why you keep doin' this to me? I was mad when I said that. You know I wouldn't do nothin' to hurt you or Simone."

"Well, Ron that may be true now, but you have done it in the past. It's hard to trust you. I'm going to let you go and Simone will be over to your mother's tomorrow."

I knew getting off the phone wouldn't be that easy.

"Lisa, do you still love me? I mean, you think we could work this out."

I sighed, "Ron, you have moved on with your life. Your mother told me about your new girlfriend who is five months pregnant. She says she's a really nice girl. It's not a question of if I love you or not, I think we have just grown apart."

He calmed down, "Getting Erica pregnant was a mistake. We were just messing around, nothing serious. I mean she's a nice girl, but I love you. I told Erica how I feel about you and Simone."

I couldn't lie to myself, I still love Ron. Even after all the abuse, betrayal and life threatening. I admitted it to him, "Ron, I do love you, but I don't know if we can rebuild what we had. Ron, if we were to be able to heal this relationship, a lot would have to change. You would have to be a contributing part of my life, not taking away from it. You would have to get your emotions together and in check. And most of all, if you thought you would be running the streets like you used to, then you need not try and come back into our lives. The only reason I'm telling you this Ron is because, it's New Year's Eve and tomorrow starts a new year with new beginnings. I'm not going backwards anymore, even if that means never seeing you again."

With sincerity in his voice, "Lisa, I've been going to anger management classes. I've also been volunteering at a battered women and children's shelter, and I realize I was out of control. I know what's important now, and maybe it took you to move and cut me off. I admit the stunt I pulled shooting myself was stupid." He began to laugh, "I really tried to shoot myself in the arm, but my mother started screaming and threw me off. I damn sho' never meant to shoot myself in the lungs."

We both laughed. For the first time, he admitted he did something. We actually had a nice talk. I promised him we could continue to communicate and take things step by step. I told him it would be a long time before we could be together. He understood and said he had all the time in the world. He knows he messed up.

Ron was the only man I had ever been with that I could tell anything to. Before we hung up, he said, "Lisa, I really do love you and I am sorry for all that I put you through. I want to be a good man, a good father and some day a good husband. I know I threw temper tantrums, but I promise to never curse in your presence or at you again. I've learned through my therapy that being spoiled by mother didn't help."

When he said that, all I could say was, "Thank you, Jesus!" He finally sees what I was telling him.

I was in tears and it was really time to hang up. He was crying and so was I.

"I'll talk to you later, Ron."

"Okay Lisa, kiss Simone for me and tell her that her daddy loves her, Happy New Year, Lisa."

"Happy New Year, Ron."

It was going on 10pm and I was trying to get to my spot. I got there around 10:30pm. I took a sit at the bar and scanned the room. Everyone had on a mask tonight again.

The half masks were the main choice, because you could still see the lips of all the members. Tonight, I wore a skin tight red dress with red heels. The dress had a v-cut down the front, which allowed for a lot of skin to show from my neck down to my navel. I was hot.

After two shots of Patron, I was ready to play a game of pool. I walked over to the pool table and set up my game. I could tell all eyes were on me. Finally, a nicely built brother came over and asked if he could join.

I politely said, "Sure, you have solids."

As we were playing he would walk past and caress my waist or hips. I was quickly getting in the mood. After missing my last shot, he came over to me and passionately kissed me. I was starting to get wet.

He bought me another shot of Patron and we finished our game. We went to the dance floor and began to dance. It was so intense and sexual that my juices were leaking down my thighs. Just before we walked off the floor, I saw her. It was the woman from the last time when I was here. She was sipping on her cocktail and watching me and this brother get into each other. Once I noticed her, she came up to us. She kissed him and then me. We were on our way upstairs to the room. It was on!

AMBER

I guess me standing my ground made Ameri decide he didn't want to lose me, because we ended up going on the trip I planned. I can't believe we had such a good time on our two day trip at Sybaris. It was nice having him all to my self for two nights and three days.

We laughed, played, and had a good time. The room was absolutely gorgeous. We had a couple of late night dips in the pool. It was wonderful.

I'm tripping though as I haven't heard from him since we came back from our little trip. I've left messages, but no return calls. I decided I need some healing, so I am going to church for New Year's Eve. I had no intentions on spending New Year's Eve with anyone but God.

I needed some answers in my life. Tonight, I'm bringing my new year in with clarity. I don't know what's going on with us or where this thing is going. I really did enjoy myself, but the

115

fun ended when we got back to Michigan and he left my house to resume our normal lives.

The good times are now only memories and this constant not knowing what's really going on is back. I guess I thought I wanted the time together to bring us closer, but it feels like it has separated more.

I can hear my cell phone ringing, but I can't find it. It's under the newspaper. I finally found it and checked the caller ID. It read: Anonymous number.

Usually I don't answer calls I can't see on caller ID, but today I decided to go ahead.

"Hello…hello!"

Finally I heard a female voice respond, "Hello."

I didn't catch the voice, "Who is this?"

She spoke in a low tone, "Hello, you don't know me, but we have a certain man in common."

I was surprised, "We do? Well, who might that be?"

She said softly, "Ameri Richards. I believe you and him are seeing each other."

I was getting pissed, "Maybe. What's it to you?"

She replied, "HE is MY husband."

I couldn't believe I was speaking to the woman who was soon to be Ameri's ex-wife. I knew sooner or later she would be trying to find out if he was seeing anybody else. I guess that trip we took pushed her to this point. I didn't want to upset her, because he told me she was a very depressed woman since the birth of their last child.

"Well, Ms. Richards, I don't know what you think you know. Maybe you need to talk to Ameri about this and not me."

She started getting a little anxious, "Look, don't play with me. I have tried to talk to Ameri, but he keeps trying to make me believe you're his brother's girlfriend. The only thing wrong with that is I know his brother is gay."

I couldn't believe it, but I knew he was trying to keep us on the down low until after his divorce was final.

"Like I said Ms. Richards, I think you are mistaken, Ameri and I are just cool."

She was getting mad, "Yeah, you two are so cool you spent two days out of town together."

I was out done. "What? I don't know what you're talking about. Please don't call my phone anymore."

She let me have it, "Look Amber, you are not the first trick Ameri has dated. Let me guess, he told you I have cancer and I'm dying. Or did he tell you we're getting a divorce? It really doesn't matter what he told you, because all you need to know is we are together and I have no plans on breaking up my family. Ameri and I have been together a long time. He is not going to leave his family. He never does. I just wanted to finally talk to you and let you know before the New Year comes in. And don't worry about tonight. He won't be able to call you because we always spend New Years Eve together, alone. So at midnight when you're wondering why he hasn't called you, it's because he is in the bed fucking his wife."

I was ready to cry and all I could do was hang up.

After hanging up the phone, I didn't know what to do. I cried for an hour. I finally got myself together enough to go to church. Nothing was going to keep me from the house of the Lord. I was dressed and on my way to Word of Deliverance. I needed some salvation.

After getting to church, I felt great walking in the door. It's something about walking in the house of the Lord that makes you feel invigorated. As always, it seems like the message for the New Year service was just for me.

I had some decisions to make. It was midnight and the service was over. The pastor told the congregation, "Happy New Year" and wished us peace, love and blessings. We could have stayed around for light snacks, but I was ready to go home. I wanted some alone time to sort out some things.

I have strong feelings for Ameri, feelings I haven't in a long time. But are they strong enough to withstand all this stress? I got his wife calling me, telling me there really is no divorce and I'm not the first woman she's found out about. As I drove from Southfield back to downtown, my mind was a hundred miles away.

I was home by 12:45am. I had showered and changed into my favorite fuzzy pajamas and curled up with a brand new journal I was starting for the New Year. My thoughts for January 1, 2006 were very emotional.

I was falling in love with a man that is legally connected to someone else. A man I've shared everything with these last six months, has probably been lying to me since day one. I've watched this stuff on Jerry Springer, not ever thinking I could be part of the cast.

It's so hard to turn your feelings off. I know I'm not going to call him. I'm going to wait for him to call me. As I sipped on a glass wine, I thought about a girl I use to work with named Havana. She told me how she had fell in love with a married man. I used to pass judgment on her and in my head, calling her a fool and stupid. Wondering how she could have ever let herself get in a situation like that.

To think, she used to ask me for advice, and I would always say leave him. Now look at me, in the same situation. I have found myself loving a married man. I can't believe it.

My pastor always says we are put in situations to learn, to be a testimony for someone else. I wonder what the lesson is going to be in this.

I wish I could see my co-worker, Havana, now. I would love to tell her, I'm sorry for judging her. That old saying of being careful how you judge somebody is so true.

I prayed for a man that cared for me and I thought I had what I wanted, but this relationship is so far from what I want. I placed my journal in my nightstand drawer and lay quietly in my bed. No television, no radio, no noise at all. Just lying there thinking.

I couldn't stop my mind from gravitating back to what his wife said to me. They're together tonight, making love for the New Year and I'm lying here thinking about it. I let out a few tears and said a prayer for strength for myself and before I closed my eyes, I thought about Havana again.

She took the buy-out in September and we kind of lost touch, but I prayed for her as well. I asked God to give me the strength to pull myself out of a situation like this. I also asked HIM to give strength to all the other women out here finding themselves in the same or similar situations. I don't know what tomorrow will bring, but December 31, 2005 was a turning point in my life.

STACY

Man, Mitch has been talking so much shit it's unbelievable. He's been trying to get me to meet him. I'm not used to him being so persistent. I guess my relationship with Mike is really getting to him. Before I could even get out the bed today, he was ringing my phone.

The jealousy Mitch is showing is kind of cool. I mean, he was always in control and making me feel my place in his life was insignificant.

Mike and I have been inseparable since the holiday break from work. The only reason why we weren't together now was because he had to help his brother move today since it's the last day of the month.

I was excited about Mike and me spending New Year's Eve together. I don't know what we were doing, but Mike said it would be wonderful. He treated me like a Princess. I never thought I would ever have anyone love me, especially anyone who knew my past.

God had blessed me, and I knew it. I just hope I won't do anything to destroy it. I hadn't been answering the phone for Mitch since I talked to him on Christmas, but I guess he wasn't going to give up.

My cell phone was ringing again, I finally decided to answer.

"Hello."

"Hey, baby girl. How you been? You a hard woman to catch up with. I've been calling you since the day after Christmas."

I knew that information already, "Well, I have been with Mike ever since the holiday." I felt so damn good saying that to Mitch. I had somebody to be with on the holiday and everyday after and somebody to be with on New Year's Eve.

That's always been the problem dating a married man; the holidays were so damn lonely. I could tell he was a little pissed.

"Yeah, well, I guess I can understand that. I haven't seen you to give you your gift. Usually you wouldn't hesitate to see me, at least to get your gift. Are you two going to be together tomorrow?"

I laughed to myself, "Not all day, he has something to do in the afternoon."

I knew he would be anxious to get some time, "Well I got to come over your way to pick up some money and then I got to head out to Madison Heights. What say you meet me at 5pm at Applebee's?"

I couldn't lie to myself, I wanted to see him. I felt stronger since I had someone I could actually call my own. I could do this and not be moved by anything Mitch would try to do.

"Okay, that sounds good. See you tomorrow."

I started packing my bag for tonight. I bought a sexy cream teddy with some thigh high stockings to match, and a pair of cream thong bikinis. I knew Mike would like that.

We have had some good sex these last few weeks. Some days better than others, so I have to give a little guidance. I hope tonight is the bomb. It just has to be on New Year's Eve.

Just as I was finishing packing my bag, I heard my mother yell up the stairs that Mike was here. He came up to my room and was looking good as ever.

He walked in and gave me a kiss, "Hey baby, you all ready?"

I smiled, "Yeah. Now are you going to tell me what we are going to do tonight?"

He smiled back, "Nope, you just have to wait and see."

I kissed my mother goodbye and we were out the door. We went to his house and he had a beautiful black gown waiting for me. He had taken the time to buy the shoes, purse, earrings, stockings, everything.

He asked me to change into this beautiful ensemble, and I did. As I exited his room, he was standing in the living room with a tuxedo on. He looked so handsome. I couldn't believe this.

He had to have planned this for weeks, because he asked me to wear my hair in an up do for New Year's and I did not think anything of it.

The door bell rang. He looked at his watch and said, "Perfect."

He told me to wait there and went out the door. Two minutes later he was back and we walked out the front door. To my surprise, a stretch Hummer Limousine was waiting for us.

The driver opened the door for me and I got in. Mike got in right behind me. There was wine chilling and two wine glasses waiting for him and I. Mike opened the bottle of wine and we headed toward a destination unknown.

Two glasses of wine and thirty minutes later, we were at the Ritz Carlton in Dearborn. This hotel was beautiful. We got on the elevator and arrived on one of the many floors of this magnificent hotel.

We were escorted through the beautiful hallway to what would be our suite for the evening. As the bell man opened the door for us and brought our luggage into the room. I was blown away by the beautiful room.

This suite was huge! It was bigger than some apartments. The design and décor was beautiful. The bathroom marble and contained a Jacuzzi tub which was filled with water and rose petals.

Mike tipped the bell man and he walked up to me, "Are you surprised?"

I still had my mouth hanging open, "Yes, I am. This is beautiful."

He went over to small sound system and Kem's A Matter of time filled the room. I felt like Cinderella.

He walked back over to me, "May I have this dance?"

I smiled, "Yes!"

We danced to Kem, Sade, and Joe Sample. This was a perfect night.

He looked me in my eyes and said, "I thought about going to a New Year's Eve party, but I realized it will be back to work soon. I wanted you all to myself so I decided we would dress up and go to a fabulous place, like this and spend the night together."

I couldn't believe it, "You did all this for me?"

"Yes baby. You're special and I love you."

There was a knock at the door. In comes room service with a cart. As the waiter removed the plates and placed them on the dining room table, Mike pulled out my chair for me to sit down. The food was wonderful.

Salmon with a hollandaise sauce, asparagus and white wine was our entrée for the evening. This night couldn't get any better. As we completed our dinner, Mike went into the bathroom to warm our water.

I couldn't wait until we made love that night. I had made up in my mind. I was going to give this my all.

I slid my evening gown off to show off the beautiful bra and panty set he had supplied me with. As we completed taking our clothes off, we slid into the warm Jacuzzi tub.

We laughed and talked and finished off our second bottle of wine. He began to wash my back and I thought of how Mitch would bathe me at his house. My mind quickly thought how good Mike's hands felt rubbing my body with his warm soap soaked hands.

I smiled briefly as I thought about how I felt young guys didn't do things like this, but Mike was a very different young man. He was caressing me and kissing me in that tub, driving me wild.

Again, there was someone knocking at our door. Mike got out the tub and put on the terry cloth robe provided for us. He returned moments later and held his hand out for me to get up and out the tub.

He began to dry my body, and stopped. "I don't want you dry, I want you wet."

He picked me up and carried me to the huge bed. Next to the bed was a bottle of champagne and chocolate covered strawberries. He laid me on the bed and began to feed me a strawberry.

We kissed and he began to suck my nipples. He moved from one to the other in perfect stride. He only paused long enough to kiss my neckline and my shoulders. Damn, he was on point tonight!

What I thought I Wanted

I was ready to explode. I wanted him so bad. I could have flipped him over on that bed and rode him like I had never ridden any man before, but part of me wanted him to make love to me.

As my eyes wandered over the room, I saw the clock approaching 11:30p.m. I knew by midnight, our bodies would be intertwined as one and we would be making love into the New Year.

Sade's 'Smooth Operator' was playing as Mike was gliding all over my body. This night was wonderful and my man had put it all together for me. I couldn't take it any longer, "Baby, I need you inside of me."

He stood up to let me see his wonderful body. My eyes focused on his manhood which clearly wanted to be inside me, but I had to taste it. I wrapped my lips around his thick and beautiful part of my man and began to give him what I knew he wanted. He moaned and looked down at me as I continued to give him pleasure.

Before I knew it he guided me to my feet and turned me around. With my ass in the air and him filling my insides up with that beautiful dick, I screamed as he entered me. He felt so good.

He leaned down to whisper, "Do you want me to make love to you or fuck you?"

With lust oozing from my mouth, "I know you love me. I need you to fuck the shit out of me!"

We were both sweating has we climaxed together. We clasped on the bed and he looked at me, "Happy New Year, Baby."

"Happy New Year, Mike. I love you."

That night we lay there in a pool of our own sweat. I loved every minute of this night. I was exhausted and satisfied. It was a New Year, January 1, 2006 and time for new changes. I just hope I was strong enough to make the beginning of a beautiful relationship with Mike and the ending of what I thought was a good relationship with Mitch.

Chapter 10

AMBER

First day of the New Year and I feel pretty good today. I decided to throw away some old things. Start anew, so to speak. I haven't heard from Ameri, but I was sure he would probably call. I wondered how his night with his wife went, and if she told him she had called me.

Just as I was wondering, my phone rang. Looking at the caller ID, I didn't have to wonder anymore because Ameri was calling.

With attitude I answered, "Hello!"

He spoke in his usual tone, "Hey Baby, how are you?"

"Ameri, you got a lot of nerve calling me after your wife called me and told me all about you."

He blurted out, "Wait a minute, my wife called you?"

"Yes, she did and she told me I'm not the first and probably won't be the last!"

"Listen, the last time I was over there watching the kids, I forgot my cell phone when I left. You were probably the last person I talked to. So that's how she was able to call you."

I didn't believe a word he said, because she knew too much.

"Look Ameri, she even knew we went out of town together."

Silence was all I heard on the other end.

Finally he opened his mouth, "I told her I was going out of town for a few days. She was just probably trying to push your buttons to see if you would give her some information. Did you tell her anything?"

I was pissed, "No Ameri. I didn't. This situation you got going on is too much for me."

He spoke in a low tone, "So what are you saying Amber? I really care about you and wanted us to be together. She is just mad that we are going through this divorce. She knew I was spending time with someone, she just didn't know who."

I guess that sounded half way believable.

"So you trying to tell me that all she said were lies."

"Yes, Amber that's what I'm saying."

I thought back to one more thing she said, "Well, if everything is a lie, where were you last night?"

He sighed, "I was over there last night, but I was watching my kids. She told me she was going out for a minute and didn't come back until 3am. Now that I think about it, she was pissed off when she left and asked me to watch the kids. I guess she had already talked to you. So that's why she stayed out, so I couldn't leave and I knew you would be mad."

Now I'm getting confused. I had this thing all figured out, but he is putting doubt in my mind.

He chimed in again, "So she had found my cell phone and went through it, but come to think of it, she supposedly found my cell phone when she came in from hanging out."

"Well, she told me at midnight you and her were fucking! What do you have to say about that? I mean, since we got back from Sybaris, you've been distant and you sure as hell haven't been sleeping with me."

He blew out even more air, "Don't you see what she is doing? She is trying to break us apart. Don't let her do this to us, Amber. Can I come over? Let's talk about this."

"Yeah, come on over Ameri. Let's say what else we need to say face to face."

We hung up and he was on his way.

The gatehouse called to let me know Ameri was here and I was ready. I was ready for anything he tried to throw at me. He came in my home looking as wonderful as ever. I did miss him.

"So, what do you have to say to me Ameri?"

127

He looked like he had lost his best friend.

"Amber, I'm sorry she called you, but she's lying to you. She is just trying to get me back and destroying what we have is part of her plan."

I softened up, "Look Ameri. I don't want to go through all this mess. I care about you. I can even admit to loving you. I have done what I said I would never do, and that is being involved with a married man. I have seen this scene and heard it play out, the ending is not good for me."

He grabbed me and hugged me.

"I know baby, but I don't want to lose you. I promise this thing will be over and we can be together. I just got to get through these court dates and be careful."

His wife's words still rang in my ear.

"So when is your first court date Ameri? I loaned you $2,000.00 for your attorney fees and you haven't so much as said a word to me about your court date."

He released me and looked like he was at a loss for words.

"I'm waiting for my court date. My attorney hasn't called me back yet."

"Okay, Amber. I gave you that money in September and it's now a New Year and you still don't have a date yet? I think you're full of shit."

He rubbed his head, "Amber, don't say that. I know what I told you, but I did go see the attorney. I'm just waiting now."

I knew that was a lie, because both my aunt and cousin went through a divorce and once they paid their money, it sure as hell didn't take four months to get a court date. Part of me still wants to believe in him.

"Do you miss me? I sure miss you."

My body was aching for him. He walked over and got so close to me I could feel his breath on my neck.

"Can I have just one kiss?"

I forced out, "No, because I know you are not coming clean with me."

He looked into my eyes, "Pleassse baby…just one kiss."

Like the sucker I knew I was becoming, I fell into a kiss that warmed my whole body and soul.

We made love and it was fantastic. He made me feel like he missed me, like he missed every inch of my body. He took his time making sure each part of my body thoroughly enjoyed him. I needed that release.

After our sexual experience, we showered together. I truly had fallen for this man. I don't know how, but here I am in one of those situations I prided myself for not getting into.

I made him a sandwich and even put some cheese on it after that love making! He sat at my dining room table enjoying his sandwich. The hours we spent together were almost perfect except his cell phone kept ringing off the hook.

Finally, he saw me getting agitated and answered the phone.

"What is it?"

I could hear her yelling at him.

"Look, I'm busy and I stayed there all night when you went out the other night. Call your mother and see if she can do it."

I heard more yelling.

"This is neither the time nor the place for me to keep talking to you about the same thing. I don't ask questions about where you are or what you're doing. You know our situation."

She must have finally said something that really pissed him off because he really started yelling.

"Look Angel! I'm not coming over there! Don't call me back and don't ask me anymore questions about where I am or who I'm with!"

He hung up. That was the first time I heard her name, Angel. At least I knew her name, considering she knew mine. I knew our peaceful time together was over. He couldn't relax anymore.

"Baby I've got to go. I'm sorry, but she just pissed me off and I need to be by myself. I'll call you later."

Just like that, he was out the door. I sat down on my sofa and started flicking through the channels. Of all things, Divorce Court was on. Judge Mablean Ephriam was giving some advice to a young lady that showed up to court with this married man, claiming she was his girlfriend.

She told the young lady, "Don't think for a minute, if he did this to his wife, he won't do it to you."

The people in the court room applauded. I reflected on my situation with Ameri and his wife. I hated saying 'wife', but that is her title in his life.

I watched the show and felt disgusted at the fact I was that girlfriend standing by my man, who is a MARRIED MAN. I cried, not because I was feeling sorry for myself. I cried because I couldn't stop my heart from loving him and wanting to be with him.

I wished I could talk to Judge Ephriam, but what good would that do? The question I had to answer for myself was do I allow myself to stay in this relationship that's going nowhere fast or cut my losses and move on? The sad thing was…I already knew the answer.

<u>LISA</u>

Ron and I have been talking more these past few weeks. I still don't trust him enough to let him take Simone by himself, but I have been dropping her over to his mother's house more.

He has gone back to work finally and has even taken me and Simone out to dinner a couple of times. It kind of feels like the old Ron is back.

I was surprised when he asked me to attend one of his anger management classes with him. It was truly an experience. His teacher told me how far Ron has come along and that he always talks about me and Simone.

I've enjoyed the time we've been spending together as a family and even the little time I've spent with Ron alone. We haven't been intimate, but it's been nice just being in his company.

I'm in a struggle with my flesh these days. I've become addicted to my spot. No wonder it's called, "Heaven on Earth."

I guess if you could go to heaven and come back, you probably couldn't wait to get back there. I always kept up with my membership and saw the doctor to make sure whenever I had the urge, I could still go there. Since I've started going back, it's harder not to go.

Plus I'm really intrigued by the woman I've been hooking up with. Sometimes I go in hopes of running into her again. Though I still love Ron, I find myself lusting for the mystery lady.

Ron asked me to go out with him for Valentine's Day. It's been a long time since I've been on a date, especially on one with Ron. Since Valentine's Day is on a Tuesday this year, Ron asked if we could go out this Saturday.

He would prefer to take me out before the day, rather than after. I decided to meet him at his Mother's house. I was dropping Simone off over there anyways and I wasn't ready for him to start coming to my new home.

I got to his Mom's house about 4p.m. He was beaming as I walked to the door with Simone.

"Hey Lisa, hey babygirl. How is the best daughter in the world?"

131

Simone was always happy to see her Daddy.

"Hi Daddy!"

His mother seemed happy to see me, or more importantly, happy to see Ron and I going out together. She came up to me and hugged me.

"Lisa, it is so good to see you. I'm so happy to see you and Ron getting alone. I hope ya'll have a good time. I heard you got a new place."

I looked at my darling little girl. All Simone could do was smile. I knew she would be the one to tell her granny about her mommy's new house. Kids will be kids.

Listening to Ms. Gladys brought me right back to when we were at the hospital, and how she prayed Ron and I would get back together. I didn't like her putting us together then, and I still don't like it now. I mean if it works out it works out, but I am not going back to Ron unless I am one hundred percent sure.

Ron was coming up in the world. He'd bought a new car and wouldn't dare ask me if I had some money. He took me to Sweet Georgia Brown downtown. This place was really nice. The restaurant was so elegant and they even had live music. I was impressed.

After being seated, Ron excused himself to go to the restroom. I stole a peek at his model type body and watched how other women were looking at him. He wore a nice gray suit and looked like he had just stepped out of the pages of GQ magazine. I instantly got heated thinking about him in a way that hadn't crossed my mind in over a year. Ron was always good looking.

Just as my imagination was going and I looked around this beautiful restaurant, my eyes fell on 'her'.

It was 'mystery lady' and she was leaving the restaurant with some guy. I couldn't see his face, but he was nicely built. Something was familiar about him. Just as she was almost out the door, she looked my way. Our eyes locked and we shared a small smile.

I was brought out of my gaze by Ron returning to the table.

He sat down and grabbed my hand, "I've been waiting for the day that we would be out to dinner again."

The waiter approached and we both decided on the fried lobster. Ron ordered a bottle of wine. The mood was very romantic.

He leaned in a little and lifted his glass. I followed suit by lifting mine as well.

He made a toast, "To new beginnings. May we look on the past as a learning experience for our future."

As our glasses touched, I was drawn to him even more. As we enjoyed the entertainment and our meals, he kept looking at me and smiling.

He put his fork down and sighed, "Lisa, I really love you. I want to show you something after we leave here."

We finished our meals and he paid for everything, including the tip. He held the door open for me to get into the car. I was impressed, two times in one day. He never opened the door for me before.

We talked as he headed west on the Jeffries. We exited the freeway and ten minutes later we were heading down a nicely manicured street. The houses were ranch style and of average size. He pulled into the driveway of one of these beautiful homes. He came around and opened my door.

Ron reached into his pocket and pulled out some keys to unlock the front door. The house was completely empty. It looked as if it had been freshly painted and the carpet appeared new. We walked through the house, which had three bedrooms and into a kitchen with new cabinets, stove and refrigerator.

The house was really nice. We ended up back in the living room.

"I want to show you the backyard."

The backyard was huge. It had a swing set with a slide and a sand box.

He walked up to me and held my face with the palms of his hands, "This is what I've been working on. I bought this house for a nice price and have been remodeling it ever since. This is my new house, and I hope one day it becomes our home."

He gently kissed me on the lips and I didn't resist. Those full lips felt so good on mine.

I slowly began to speak, "Ron...we need to talk..."

Before I could finish my sentence he interrupted, "I know this will not happen overnight, but I want my family back."

"What about Erica? I know you said getting pregnant wasn't supposed to happen, but she is and it's your baby. We have enough problems as it is, we definitely don't need baby mama drama added to it."

He looked so sincere, "I know Lisa. I have been talking to Erica. I told her I will pay child support, but WE don't have a future as a couple. We got together because I was hurting from my break up with you and she was hurting from a break up with some dude. We just comforted each other. I can't lie and tell you that she doesn't want more, but I've been stern and assured her there will be nothing else but the love for our child that we will share."

We got back in the car and the ride back to his mother's house was quiet. I had a lot to think about. This new Ron was blowing my mind. He was taking the steps to show me he was ready to get his life together and he wanted it to include me.

A big part of me was ready to move forward, but certain parts were scared to try. I mean Ron had done so much in our past. The threats, the violence, even the shooting.

It was so much, but part of me loved this man, really loved him. Not just because he was the father of my most precious possession, but because Ron always understood me.

Truth be told, the bisexual me was able to evolve with Ron. We always wanted to have a threesome back some years ago. So one year, it was his birthday, and we went to AllStars. Now AllStars was a strip club and he had asked me a thousand times before to go with him.

On his birthday, I had planned everything. I had arranged for a special table to be set-up and paid for him some lap dances and I had some as well. I was so turned on by the whole atmosphere. I couldn't believe I was feeling this way.

After we got nice and toasted, we left AllStars and went to the Residence Inn in Southfield. I had one of the strippers meet us there and it was on!

After being introduced to that lifestyle, I was hooked. I think I enjoyed Ron's birthday more than he did. The stripper and I exchanged numbers and over a six month span, I couldn't cut her loose.

She even wanted me to leave Ron! And the crazy thing was that I actually contemplated it. He really didn't mind me hooking up with her, as long as he could be a part of it. Once he found out I was seeing her without him, he demanded I leave her alone. She was the one who introduced me to the spot.

After Ron protested about me seeing the stripper, I finally stopped and told her my family was more important. I couldn't put my daughter through her mom dating a woman and leaving her daddy. She understood.

Sometimes we ran into each other at the spot and we still hooked up. I was only visiting the spot once a month and as time went on I went less and less back then. Now, I have been rejuvenated and I've been going there a lot lately. I feel so relaxed when I'm there.

As we pulled in front of his mother's house, I looked over at him and wondered if I could give up the intriguing woman at the spot. She was in my dreams and I wanted her all the time. I really had some decisions to make and the thought process would be long. Would I give up my comfortable lifestyle this time for my family or give into what my flesh totally wanted?

That night, I picked up my daughter and placed her in the car.

I turned to face Ron as he said, "Just think about giving our family one more try. I promise you won't be disappointed."

I smiled and kissed him softly on his lips.

"I'll call you when I get home, Ron."

Never responding to his last comment, I got in the car and was on my way home.

Simone called out from the backseat, "Mom, are you and daddy getting back together?"

I smiled and looked at her through the rearview mirror, as thoughts of the mystery lady flashed through my head, "We'll see baby…we'll see."

KIM

My New Year was off to a great start. I have a great new man in my life who takes up time with my son, and my son adores him. Alan was such an attentive man. Some days, I would be so exhausted with work and school I would awake to him massaging my feet. He would cook dinner for me and Malcolm, and he had even taught Malcolm how to drive.

I was on my way home from work and stopped by the Post Office to check my P.O. Box. I have been keeping a P.O. Box since moving to Michigan, just so my home address was not used for all my business matters.

I made sure work, credit card companies, and other business used that address. After pulling out my mail, I sat in the car thumbing through the envelopes. I came across a strange envelope with no return address. I opened it up and recognized the handwriting immediately.

I was shaking as I began to read, *"Hi Justine, I mean Kim. It's taken me a long time to find you but surprise! I got to get use to your new name. You did a good job of hiding. I mean, it's been years. It's amazing what a little money can do for you. Thanks to my dad, he left me set for life when he died. My Mother cashed in all the savings bonds and stocks he had purchased for me and I have enough money to never have to work, so the police can't arrest me.*

Like you, I have a new name and new life. I see you've done well for yourself, my son has gotten big. He looks a lot like my dad. I've been watching you from a far for a long time, and would have never exposed myself until I started seeing this guy picking my son up from school, spending the night with you, taking my place. I can't have that.

As much as I know I was wrong for what I did to you Justine…there I go again, Kim, I don't want another man raising my son. When the time is right, I will be standing right before you. You will leave him alone and let him go back to his life as a single personal trainer, or I will have to end it for you.

I tried to kill you before, but this time, I will succeed. As for my son, I brought him in this world so I don't mind taking him out. Even though I got a lot of money now, my life is lonely. I need my family. Be careful Kim, you never know where I'll be.

I know you going to go to the police and probably the FBI, but I really don't care. You know, I used to think money would solve all my problems, but I now realize it doesn't. I'll be in touch real soon. Joseph."

I dropped the letter in my lap and began to cry. I thought I would never have to use the FBI number I was given when I started my life over, but I have to protect Malcolm from this maniac.

I raced home and dug through all my old papers and found the card. I read the name. "Ed Matthews." It felt like it was only yesterday when Agent Matthews helped me to begin a new life. I hoped he still worked there.

As the phone rang on the other end, my heart was pounding. Finally someone answered, "FBI, Special Agent Matthews speaking."

"Mr. Matthews, you may not remember me, but you helped me start my life over some years ago. My new name is Kim Mitchell."

He chimed in, "Yes, Ms. Mitchell. I can't forget you and little Malcolm. To what do I owe this pleasure? Usually when someone calls me after so long, it's not good news."

He couldn't be more right.

"I am afraid Mr. Matthews, I've been contacted by Joseph. I have a very disturbing letter he sent to my P.O. Box and I am afraid for Malcolm and I. He said he doesn't have a problem killing us. What do I do?"

"Well, first of all I am on the next flight out of here and I will be arriving in Detroit some time tonight. I need that letter, can you fax it to me?"

"Yes, I have a fax machine at home. Give me the number." I dialed the number as he recited it to me. "It should be coming through."

"Yes, I hear the fax machine."

He was quiet for a couple of minutes.

"Mr. Matthews, are you there?"

"Yes. Give me a number where I can call you back. I will call you back in less than ten minutes."

Ten minutes felt like ten hours. I called Alan while I was waiting and asked him to get over here as fast as he could.

He kept asking, "Baby what's the matter?"

"I'll tell you when you get here, and pick up Malcolm for me."

I hung up and called Malcolm's cell phone to tell him that Alan would pick him up.

He got upset, "Ma, I'm at practice and the coach is going to be pissed if I leave."

"Look Malcolm, this is some serious shit. Now do what I said!"

He'd never heard me curse so he knew this was serious, "Okay Ma, I'll be waiting for Alan."

Soon as I hung up the phone, Agent Matthews called back.

"Ms. Mitchell, I have my flight all set. I'll be there within the next three hours. Give me your address."

After hanging up the phone, I sat down on my sofa and waited for everyone to get there. I called work and called off for the next day, because I knew I wasn't going there tomorrow. I called Malcolm's counselor and told her he would not be at school tomorrow.

As I sat in silence, I prayed, "Lord, I can't believe this is happening to me. I know you won't put more on me than I can bear. Lord, give me the strength to fight this demon and protect my son. I ran before Lord, this time help me to fight to sustain my life. I believe in you Father, it's time to defeat the devil. Amen."

By seven o'clock, everyone had arrived. Agent Matthews briefed Malcolm and Alan about the situation because I was too upset to speak.

He spoke very stern, "Malcolm you and your mother have been in witness protection. Mr. Williams, Ms. Mitchell has explained to me that you are a very important part in her life and as a safety precaution for her and her son, I need some information on you just to do a background check."

Alan didn't hesitate, "I'll give you whatever you need. I just want Kim and Malcolm to be safe."

Agent Matthews continued, "I understand and appreciate your cooperation. Now, Kim, I need to give you some information. I have set up surveillance around Joseph's mother's house and we have a wire tap going in to her home tomorrow. We have started a search on Joseph and have links to Spain, Jamaica, and here in Michigan. He has more than one identity and could be anywhere. You have heard of America's Most Wanted?"

I was surprised to hear Agent Matthews say that, "Yes, I watch the show all the time."

"Well, we need to air your story and put Joseph's face across every television set in the United States."

I really didn't want to do that, but I knew it was best.

"Agent Matthews, I will do whatever it takes to secure my home, family and loved ones. I want to be clear, I am not running anymore. I will not change my identity again and I will not move. I deserve a life and so does my son. So whatever we have to do, let's get it going."

Agent Matthews smiled, "I'm glad you feel that way. The crew will be here tomorrow to see you and it will air this Saturday. We have to get on this as soon as possible. In the meantime, you will have undercover officers' following you, Malcolm and even Mr. Williams. This is for your protection."

After Agent Matthews finished briefing us, he told me he would see me first thing tomorrow.

Later on that evening Alan and I lay in my bed speechless. I was lost in my own thoughts and I'm sure he had a lot on his mind as well.

He finally broke the silence, "Baby, you know I love you, right?"

I looked at him, "Yes baby."

"I've waited a long time to meet a woman like you and I am willing to fight for you. I just want you to know, I'm not going nowhere. I plan on being with you for the rest of our lives."

Tears formed in my eyes and I spoke softly, "And I plan on being with you Alan. I can't run anymore. I love you too much to give up what we have for someone who hasn't been a part of my life or my son's. You have given us more than he ever could or has. I love you and I'm willing to fight for you."

We kissed and held each other until we fell asleep. I woke up from a nightmare and looked over at Alan. He was sound asleep. I walked into the kitchen and Malcolm was sitting at the table.

"Hey honey. What you doing up?"

He was reading the paper, "I can't sleep Mom. I can't believe he is trying to harm us. Why won't he just go away?"

"Honey, your father was always controlling and I'm sure he hasn't changed. He was worse on drugs."

He looked up at me with anger in his eyes, "Mom, I'm going to protect you. You protected me all these years and now it's my turn. Mom, I want you to know, I am not going to let him harm you. I love you so much Mom."

He got up from table and hugged me tight.

I fought back my tears and told my baby, "I appreciate every thing you said, but you are MY SON and I love you. I will fight to the bitter end for you. If your dad comes here, God as my witness, the only way he leaving is in a body bag."

STACY

I got a message from Kim. She wants me to come over to her house on Saturday. She has something she wants to tell me and the rest of the girls. I hope everything is alright. Life is going so good for Kim. She finally has a good man in her life and she deserves it.

I know I'm doing something fucked up right now. I'm getting ready to meet Mitch. He's been calling and begging. I know he's seeing this new girl at work, but it really don't bother me.

I used to be pissed when I found out he had another young girl around the plant. I guess I'm getting over him. I just can't seem to cut the ties all the way.

I was on my way to his house and feeling kind of bad. Mike has been all that I need, but yet I'm still going to see Mitch. Before I left work, Mike told me he was working overtime all this week. He's been working a lot of overtime. I hope he don't think he has to do that for me. He is so good to me. What we have is so much bigger than money. I never thought I would say that about anybody.

I got to Mitch's house in thirty minutes. I parked in my usual spot. I got to the door and he was waiting for me.

"Hey sweet thang. I've been missing you."

I half-heartedly smiled and walked in.

"How you doing Mitch?"

He shut the door and looked back at me, "Is that the way you greet your man?"

"Mitch don't start acting brand new. You know you are not my man and I'm not your woman."

I walked over to him and gave him an unenthused hug.

"Damn baby, you don't seem like you miss your daddy. I know we ain't had the best relationship, but we had some good times. Come on wash your hands, I fixed dinner."

I went into the bathroom to wash my hands and heard his telephone ringing. I walked out the restroom.

"Aren't you going to answer that?"

"Nah, it ain't for me."

I sat down to my favorites, shrimp scampi and wild rice.

"Mitch, what you trying to do? Where's your spouse?"

He sat down, "She just left for the airport. She's going to visit her sister in Mississippi."

I was sitting there listening to his conversation and couldn't stop thinking about Mike. After finishing dinner, I knew what was next, but I wasn't feeling that with Mitch. Mike had been working so hard to please me and our sex life was pretty good.

"Mitch, I want to talk to you."

He smiled, "Well, let's talk after you get this money."

I knew what that meant. I started thinking about how I had been degrading myself all this time. I suddenly felt so stupid.

"Why don't you go upstairs and see what I got for you up there."

Mitch was cleaning up the kitchen and just as I was getting ready to open the gift on the bed, I heard his front door open.

I heard a woman's voice call out, "Mitch where you at?"

I heard him moving fast to the front door, "Hey baby, what you doing back?"

"They cancelled my flight, so I can't leave until tomorrow. What you doing?"

"Ohh! I just got finish making me some dinner and was about to go over my buddy Charlie's house to play some cards."

I heard her say, "Well I'll see you when you get back. I'm going to take a nap."

I was shivering in my boots as I listened to the scene unfolding.

Before she could get to the steps, I heard him say, "Why don't you sit down and let me fix you something to eat."

I was scared shitless! I thought back to my girls always telling me this shit was going to happen. I guess they were right.

I heard his wife yell, "What the hell you trying to pull Mitchell? You had somebody in my house?"

He started stuttering, "Nah baby. Why you say some shit like that?"

"Because it's lipstick on one of my wine glasses, and if you aren't a cross dresser, that mean somebody has been here or is still here!"

I heard the kitchen chair move and she was stomping through the house.

"Where the fuck is she? I told your old ass if I found out you been having someone in my house, I'm going to make your life Hell!"

I could tell she was going from room to room. I was backing up and stumbled over his slippers.

"Oh, she upstairs…in my room, ah, hell naw!"

I heard her coming up the stairs and had to think fast. I opened the balcony doors that were off their room and shut them quietly. Thank good they had one of those two tier decks so I ran down the stairs. I heard her throwing shit, opening and closing doors. She was going crazy. I couldn't blame her. I pulled my car keys out my pants pocket and headed to my car. I jumped in and pulled off slowly.

I was breathing so hard, I thought my heart was going to come through my chest. I knew I was playing with fire. All those times I went there and slept with him. God was trying to show me a long time ago, now He's trying to beat some sense in my head. This situation could have been way worse. One of us could be dead right now.

As I was driving, I realized I didn't have my purse. Oh my God, I left my purse by the television in his bedroom. She will have my identification, where I stay, my work ID, everything. Oh Shit! I can't turn back. I was driving so fast on the freeway, you would have thought I was in a high speed chase.

I called Amber, I had to call somebody. She answered on the first ring.

"Hello?"

"Hey Amber. Ohmigod! Girl I went over to Mitch's house and his wife came home!"

She screamed, "Oh no! Are you okay?"

"Yeah, but I left my purse. She is going to know who I am!"

"Damn Stacy. I told your ass to stop going over there."

I didn't want to hear that shit right now, "Yeah, so did everybody else! What am I going to do?"

Amber spoke calmly, "First you got to try and calm down. Maybe she hasn't seen it yet. It's really nothing you can do other than wait for him to call. I know he's going to call you."

I was so upset, "This was the dumbest shit I've done. I went there to tell him, I'm not going to see him anymore. From the moment I walked in the door, I felt like I shouldn't be there."

My other line clicked, it was Mitch. I told Amber I would call her back.

As soon as I clicked over, he started talking, "Baby girl, I didn't know she was coming back. I thought she was long gone. You okay?"

I was pissed, "Yeah, I'm okay but I left my purse."

He cut me off, "I know. I found it before she did. I got it with me. Can you meet at the Residence Inn on Ford Road?"

I got even madder, after being damn near caught up his old ass is still trying to get some booty.

"I can meet you Mitch, but it will only be to get my purse. This is enough for me to realize I need to leave your ass alone. I shouldn't have ever started coming to your house in the first place. Just because you didn't give a damn, I should have thought more of myself."

He was trying to get a word in, "Stacy, baby. Look, I know…I shouldn't have been playing thangs that close. I really do care about you. I just been with Jude for so long and if I would divorce her, she'd get half my pension."

I was so angry at him.

"So your happiness is based on your pension? Mitch, you are a hustler. You make so much money out in the streets. I know you do because I've helped you do your books. So stop bullshitting me!"

I never heard him sound so beaten down, "Stacy, it could never work with me and you in the real world. Look at me and look at you. You know people wouldn't accept us."

"Mitch, I don't want to talk about this anymore. I will see you at the hotel."

I pulled up at the hotel and Mitch was already there. He motioned for me to follow him. I couldn't believe he was still trying to get some ass. I couldn't wait until we pulled over. I got out the car in a rage.

"Can I have my shit, PLEASE!?"

He looked nervous, "Can you at least come in and talk to me?"

I smacked my lips, "Hurry up as I motioned toward the room door."

Once inside, he started that same ol' bullshit again.

"Baby girl, I don't want to lose you. I know I've been an ass at times, but you never acted like you cared."

Mitch knew I cared about his ass. He was just trying anything.

"Look Mitch, I'm getting too old for this and I need some stability in my life. Evidently, you can't give it to me, so I'm moving on. I care about you but, caring is not enough anymore."

He looked so broken.

"Stacy, I thought you would always be around for me. Whether you believe it or not, I look at you more than just a piece of ass."

I believed him, but I have a man that really loves me and I would be a fool to let him go to be somebody else's second choice.

"Mitch, I have enjoyed our time together, but it's time we part ways as friends. I will always be your friend, but nothing more."

He looked at me, "I understand. Can I at least have a hug before you go?"

I hugged Mitch and walked out that room feeling good about myself. I had finally made a decision that felt right. I couldn't wait to see Mike and tell him how much I loved him.

Chapter 11

KIM

I got in touch with all my girls and they should be here shortly. I told everyone to be here at 8:30pm and not to be late. I asked Lisa, Stacy and Amber to come alone because what I had to say, I didn't want to share with anyone else.

Alan was in the kitchen making some gumbo and corn bread for our guests. I had the television tuned into channel 2 for America's Most Wanted.

They all got to my house on time. We hugged and I asked them to be seated in the living room. Alan came into the living room.

I introduced him, "Ladies, this is Alan. I know you've heard a lot about him, I'm glad you finally got to meet him."

Alan spoke and sat down.

Lisa couldn't wait, "Kim you got us all scared as hell. I picked everyone up to make sure we were here on time."

I could always count on Lisa.

"Okay, remember how you guys are always asking me about my past and I've always been so evasive?"

They all nodded yes.

"Well, that's because my past was something I was trying to forget."

For the next fifteen minutes I explained my relationship with Joseph and how I left Chicago to move here. I explained about the witness protection program Agent Matthews had placed me in. My friends looked on in amazement. Finally I introduced Agent Matthews.

"Ladies this is Agent Matthews. We brought you here to watch my story air on America's Most Wanted. Joseph sent me a letter, a very threatening letter. He didn't finish what he sat out to do a long time ago, so he is threatening Malcolm and me. He is basically saying if I don't leave Alan, then he will end our relationship himself."

Lisa had started to cry and Stacy jumped up with an attitude, "Fuck that punk. We just gonna have to stay here with you. When his bitch ass come, we gonna lay his ass out!"

Amber walked over to me and hugged me, she spoke softly, "I love you Kim and we will get through this. Whatever you need us to do, we will be here."

She looked at Lisa and Stacy and they came over to me. We all hugged for what seemed like ages. I am so blessed to have friends like these.

We sat down when America's Most Wanted came on. We all sat there quietly, watching so intensely. John Walsh introduced my story and said it was an "all points bulletin" out for Joseph McAfee. As they did the dramatization of my story, I couldn't help but cry. I never really felt it like that before.

I rubbed my legs and arms, feeling the scars left from Joseph's attack on me. Alan came over to me and rubbed my back as we continued to watch.

My interview came up, and I was glad I spoke out against Joseph. My face was distorted, so people wouldn't know it was me. I made it clear that I was going to protect my son and me with every ounce of strength I have in my body. The FBI even moved Joseph's name up to the ten most wanted list and John Walsh said he may be in the metropolitan Detroit Area.

Once my story was over, Lisa was so shaken up. I guess because my story hit closer to home for her. I asked her to follow me into the kitchen just as we finished watching the man hunt for a serial killer. As we walked into the kitchen, I looked at my friend.

"Don't be scared for me. I'm going to be alright. Malcolm is going to be alright."

She smiled through the tears, "That's why you were so afraid for me?"

149

I smiled, "Yes, see Ms. Mary was the lady who saved my life. She wanted me to tell you my story a long time ago, but I just couldn't do it. I guess because I didn't want to bring up the past. God has a way of making us deal with things."

She reached out and held my hand, "Kim, I don't want to lose you. You have been my very best friend. I'm with Stacy, We gonna beat his ass!"

We both laughed and went back into the living room to join everybody else.

Surprisingly, my girls all stayed the night. We camped out in the living room talking, laughing, and sometimes crying. We listened to old school music and did some old school dances. Malcolm and Alan had fun with us for awhile, but then went to play the Xbox.

God, who would have known that Joseph could bring us together like this? We never took the time to bond like this. I mean, we hung out and drank, but never real conversations like this.

We all shared something with each other that night. Amber told us how she loves Ameri, but deep down she knows the relationship isn't right. Lisa told us how Ron was getting help and he had bought a new house. I was happy that he was moving in the right direction. She said he even took her out to dinner for a change and she didn't have to pay for anything. Stacy finally admitted what we all knew for years, that she loved Mitch's old ass, but not enough to risk losing Mike. Mitch is her past and Mike is her future. We all clapped on that one.

Lisa looked around at all of us and took a deep breath.

She asked us, "Guys, you love me no matter what right?"

We all looked at each other, "Right!"

She took a deep breath, "Well, I feel like I can tell ya'll this…I mean you are my family."

We were all still puzzled.

She started in again, "Please don't love me any less."

I looked at her, "We won't, right ladies?"
They again chimed in, "Right!"
Lisa reluctantly started to speak, "I'm…I'm bisexual."

LISA

Kim dropped a bomb on us. I would have never known she had been through that much. I always thought those scars she had came from falling through a window as a child. At least that's what she told me, but I guess she wouldn't want to say "My baby daddy tried to stab me to death."
After she told us about her situation, I felt compelled to be honest with my friends who are like my family. I was hoping for some insight from them.

I explained how I love Ron, but I have a thing for women as well. I told him how I got started into that lifestyle, but they just listened and never judged me.

I was surprised to hear Amber speak up and talk about her experimentation with women. I never would have guessed that from her. She made me feel the most comfortable. I guess because she could sympathize with me on a deeper level.

After we finished off a couple bottles of wine and some purple passion, we were all feeling real good. We laughed and cried into the wee hours of the morning. I don't know who fell asleep first, but we woke up to the smell of breakfast.

Kim's new man is awesome. He made us pancakes, eggs and bacon that morning and it was right on time! I am happy for Kim. She really is my best friend. God has blessed me with some great people.

We all vowed we would be there for Kim and Malcolm. If she was staying here in Michigan and fighting for her life, then we were with her.

Amber is supposed to be coming over to my house today. I guess she wants to talk a little more about my situation.

151

"Mama, what time is Auntie Amber coming?"

My little girl is so inquisitive.

"She will be here soon, baby."

Simone went back to her room and I continued to clean up around my new place. I was cleaning up when my phone rang.

"Hey Lisa. How you doing?"

It was Ron.

"I'm fine."

"How'd your night go with the girls?"

I smiled, "It went good. Amber is on her way over here to spend some time with Simone."

He sighed, "Oh…I was hoping to spend some time with you two today."

I wanted to spend sometime with him as well.

"Well, she probably won't be here for a long time. I'll call you after she leaves, okay?"

"Okay, tell my angel daddy said hello."

I called Simone to the phone, "Simone! Your daddy wants to talk to you!"

She ran towards the phone and grabbed it, "Hi Daddy! What you doin'?"

I heard her say yes a couple of times and told her daddy she loved him.

"Here Mommy, "she handed me the phone.

"Okay Ron, I'll call you in a couple of hours."

The door bell rang and Simone raced to the door.

"It's Auntie Amber! Auntie Amber!"

I opened the door and Amber and I hugged. She picked up Simone and gave her a hug. Simone was so excited she could barely contain herself.

"Auntie, I want to show you my new dolls my Mommy and Daddy bought me!"

After Amber put her down, Simone grabbed her hand and pulled her toward her bedroom. They must have been back there for an hour, while I finished my cleaning.

Amber came out of the room, "Girl, Simone is a trip. She talked to me until she fell asleep."

We sat down and I poured her a glass of white wine.

"So what's up with you and Ameri?"

"Girl, I don't even know what's up with Ameri. When we spend time together, it's great…but then there is always his wife that's involved."

Now that threw me for a loop, I didn't know he had a wife.

"He's married Amber!"

She looked at me with those puppy dog eyes, "He's going through a divorce…well, I think he is."

Now I'm really confused.

"Is he going through a divorce or not?"

"Well he borrowed some money from me to start the proceedings."

I shook my head, "Amber, now I know you a smart woman. You and I both know that sounds like a bunch of bull shit."

She smacked her lips, "Yeah, it is hard to believe ain't it? Not to mention I talked to his wife."

This girl is going to give me a heart attack, I swear.

"You talked to his wife? What did she have to say?"

"She told me Ameri wasn't going anywhere and he had done this before. She even told me not to worry where he was going to be on New Year's because, he was going to be in the bed with her. You know what Lisa? He didn't call me New Year's Eve either."

She started crying and I felt so sorry for her.

"Amber, it's going to be okay. I think you need to move on. Let Ameri get his divorce or whatever he is going to do and if you're still single and he's single, then you see if you guys can start a relationship. You can not start a relationship like this, at least not a good one."

She tried to dry her eyes, "I love him Lisa. He makes me feel so good when we're together."

I looked at her, "Girl, that's what the married man is supposed to do. You talk to Stacy about this?"

She reluctantly said, "Yeah…we been driving by his house."

"Oh my God, can it get any worse? Driving by for what?"

"Just to see if he's lying to me when he says he's not there."

I couldn't resist, "Is he?"

"Yeah Lisa, he is there sometimes when he says he's not."

I shook my head again, "Amber this is too much. You owe yourself so much more than this."

"I know Lisa, I just don't know what to do. I'm not ready to let him go."

I looked at her, "Girl you need to get out and mingle. Meet some new people."

She was with that, "You right, but I don't know where to go. I wish I could go back to those earlier days in college when we would go to one of our friends' apartments, get drunk and do whatever…those where the days. That's when I was experimenting with the same sex. We were loose, carefree and whatever we did stayed amongst us."

I smiled at her because I had a spot like that right here in the city.

"Well we need to go out."

She looked at me, "Yeah, but where , some old club? The club scene ain't for me."

I held her hand, "Amber I know just the spot."

AMBER

I was getting dressed to hang out with Lisa. I decided to call Kim to check on her. She's been such a strong person through her ordeal. The rest of the girls and me make sure we call her everyday.

Two weeks have passed and this Joseph character hasn't showed up yet. I guess that's good and bad. Good because Kim is still living her life, bad because someone is still out on the streets that wants to end her life.

"Hey Kim, how you doing?"

"Fine girl. I just got in from getting some groceries. Getting ready to cook a little dinner for my guys."

I was happy to hear she was doing okay considering all things.

"Well, I just wanted to check on you. I'll probably talk to you tomorrow. Tell Alan and Malcolm I said 'Hello'."

I could tell Kim was smiling, "He's standing right here, I'll tell him. I love you Amber."

"I love you too Kim."

I was getting ready when the phone started ringing. I smacked my lips because I knew who it was.

"What's up, Ameri?"

"Hey baby. I wanted to come through."

"I'm getting ready to go out."

I knew I had shocked his ass with that one. It felt so damn good to have something else to do other than sitting at home waiting on him to get free.

"Going out where?" he asked.

No he didn't just ask me where! He has a lot of nerve.

"I'm going out with Lisa to some club."

He seemed like he had an attitude after he heard that.

"Oh, so you clubbing now? Any other time you would be glad to spend some time with me. Now you'd rather be out with your girl."

I really did want to spend some time with him. I even thought about canceling with Lisa and staying at home to see Ameri.

"What time are you talking about coming through, Ameri?"

"Well, I'm waiting on her to get back and then I'll be on my way."

Here we go again. That was enough to get my mind back right. It's been so many times I've waited all night for his wife to get back home and she never does. Or there is some other reason like she got in so late he didn't want to wake me. I don't know what kind of work she does but she sure keeps some late hours.

I don't know if I want to take that chance with him tonight. It seems Ms. Angel comes in late or not at all to just keep Ameri at their house.

"Ameri, I've heard that before. You never seem to make it when you are waiting on her. I need to get out of this house. All I do these days is wait to see if you're coming over. Call me when she gets home, and maybe I'll be done hanging out with my girl."

I knew he was pissed. I was holding my breath after I said that shit to Ameri. I knew he was going to come back with something.

"Oh, so since I can't come right now, you're going out? Okay Amber, have a good time. I'll call you later on. I'm not going to trip because I know I'm still married and you are single woman. I ain't going to play like I ain't jealous or mad that other guys is gonna be checking you out, but it ain't nothing I can do about that."

I was relieved and kind of happy that he was jealous. I didn't want to stay on the phone because it wasn't anything else left to say.

"I'll talk to you later on tonight."

"Yeah! Bye!"

I felt bad in some ways, but sitting at home was depressing. My phone rang again. Lisa was at the gatehouse and I was out of here!

I jumped in the car with Lisa and she was looking pretty hot. When she got all girly, she was the bomb. I'd always thought she was attractive, but I wasn't going that route. I left that lifestyle back in college.

She was being all mysterious when I asked where we were going. She smiled at me and said, "Some place where you can be yourself."

My curiosity was peaked.

"Is it a club?"

She smirked, "Yeah, a members-only club, very exclusive club. Not too many people know about this place."

We arrived at the 'club' and the parking lot was jammed. We walked in and it was off the chain! There were a lot of people in here. As we walked through the crowd towards the bar, I was getting looks from both men and women. I started to wonder what I had walked in to.

I could tell Lisa was comfortable. Once we got to the bar, she must have known the fine ass bartender, because he leaned over the bar and kissed her.

She ordered us two purple passions and we both canvassed the room. We walked over to the pool table because Lisa challenged me to a game. I started racking up the balls and Lisa was strutted her stuff.

My sister looked good in her black mini-skirt and off the shoulder sheer blouse. I couldn't help but notice her nipples were hard and showing through that black sheer shirt.

As I was looking at Lisa, I noticed her eyes where fixed on something. I followed her stares to an attractive sister at the bar. I instantly knew they had a connection. Lisa couldn't even get her game on!

The woman walked over to the pool table just as Lisa was taking her shot. The woman grabbed the ball as it glided across the table and walked up to Lisa and started kissing her.

I was standing there with my mouth open feeling envious and shocked at the same time. I wanted to feel that passion.

They broke their kiss and the woman said something to Lisa. Lisa motioned for me to come over to them. I walked over to them not knowing what to expect.

I knew I was looking fly tonight. I had on a pair of Chanel riding boots, a bustier top and my black fitted Seven jeans.

Once I approached them, Lisa didn't call me by my name, she just introduced me as 'her girl'. I spoke and we smiled at each other. The woman asked if I would mind if she kissed me. I got instantly wet as I shook my head 'no' giving this sexy ass stranger permission to kiss me. Lisa smiled and the woman kissed me. It was so passionate and steamy. Several people began to gather around us as we all started kissing on another.

Finally a well built brother came up and asked if we wanted to take this upstairs. I didn't know what he meant by that, but evidently Lisa and the woman did. They walked towards a staircase leading upstairs.

Before I could follow behind them, the good looking brother grabbed my hand, "Wait, I want to get to know you."

For the next fifteen minutes this brother and I made out at a small table in the corner. I needed this type of attention.

Ameri hasn't been giving me anything lately. We haven't been spending much time together, because he always has something to do. When we do see each other, the sex isn't as passionate as it was when we first got together.

I mean he still does it for me, but the quality of time together is horrible. Either Ameri doesn't make it over, or he has to leave right after we make love.

As this handsome brother kissed my neck and pulled my breasts out of my bustier to suck them, I thought I was going to cum right there. After he finished his business, he pulled my bustier back over my breasts and asked if I wanted to go upstairs.

I sat there for a moment trying to find my voice.

"This is my first time here. My friend brought me here to get out the house. I don't know anything about upstairs."

He smiled at me, "Well, let me explain. This is a members' only club. We are a group of men and women who are tested for STD's and we come here to fulfill our sexual urges.

Whether we want to be with the opposite sex or the same sex, the choice is ours without prejudice. Your friend must really trust you. The first time, you come for free and after that you must join and go through the testing procedure to continue to indulge."

Wow, this place was great! Sex without rules or relationship...just getting your freak on and go home.

After I thought about it I said, "I would love to go upstairs."

The bedroom was tasteful. Like a hotel room. Once in the room, he stripped me of my clothes and asked me to have a seat. He stripped slowly, never taking his eyes off of me. I looked at every inch of his body. He was gorgeous. Finally he took off his Calvin Klien boxers to expose his manhood. It was enormous and I wanted it.

As he walked over to me to lay me down, I had to taste it. I wrapped my lips around this extraordinary piece that my mouth couldn't seem to handle. Well, not at first I couldn't. I could always control my gag reflex and I took care of him like a woman should take care of a man.

After he came all over me, he took me into the bathroom, where he washed me up in the shower. We went back into the room and he started to kiss and caress my body. He put those full lips between my thighs and kissed my wet lips. Oh my God! This is amazing.

After he made me cum, he turned me over onto my knees and it was time for insertion. He was a freak and I loved it.

He asked me, "You think you can handle what I got to give you?"

I couldn't wait to feel the pain, "As long as it hurts so good!"

He started to put that magnificent piece of work inside of me and I thought I was going to die. It hurt so good. He was going slow, and then fast and hard. Finally we came together and fell onto the bed.

After we showered again and were putting our clothes on, I noticed he was still staring at me.

"Why are you staring at me?"

He smiled, "I like you."

I was flattered, but not stupid, "I bet you say that to all the girls you do the first time you meet them."

He shook his head, "No, this hasn't happened to me in a long time, but I was so attracted to you. I wanted to know you."

I was flattered again, but last time I met a man who was so drawn to me, he was married with problems.

"I don't know how this works, but I did enjoy myself."

He laughed, "It works like you want it to. Can I ask you something?"

"Sure."

He kneeled down as I sat on the rumpled bed.

"Would you like to go out with me? I enjoyed what we did tonight, but I would like to get to know you better."

Wow, I couldn't believe he was asking me out. But there was a flashing light in my head that I couldn't help but to address.

"I have to ask, are you married? Going through a divorce, or living with someone?"

He laughed so hard, "I'm not mad at you, and to answer your questions no, no, and no."

I smiled, "Well, I'm Amber and you are?"

He smiled and rose to his feet, "My name is Carrington, and I am so very pleased to meet you Amber. So can I take you out Sunday for brunch?"

"Sunday for brunch will be fine."

I wrote my number down and he gave me his home number and cell number. That was impressive in itself.

We went back downstairs and Lisa was sitting at a small table talking to the mystery woman. She saw me coming and we were out the club.

The ride home was great. All we talked about was our sex-capades. What Lisa said next shocked me, "My girl was interested in you. She wanted to do a threesome."

I smiled at the thought, "I'm not ready for that Lisa. Right now, all I see and smell on my body is Carrington. I don't want nothing else but that man."

161

Chapter 12

<u>LISA</u>

I'm trying to layoff my spot, because I want to try and work this thing out with Ron. Erica had her baby about two weeks ago and I was sure he was going to flip on me, but he hasn't.

He goes to see his child and has been supportive to Erica and the baby. He even picked her up from the hospital, which I told him was the right thing to do.

I've even been helping out, because the girl doesn't have a job. She is on welfare, but the baby needs so much.

I took Simone to JC Penney's and we shopped for her baby brother some clothes. She was so excited. I didn't want to hurt Erica's feelings or offend her so I just dropped the clothes off to Ron's mother's house.

I was surprised when Ron called me and said Erica wanted to speak to me. As I suspected, she was ghetto.

"Hey, how you doin'?"

"Alright, how are you?"

She was popping her bubble gum and irritating the hell out of me but I held my cool.

"I'm awright…I preciate you buyin' clothes and stuff for LaRon. I know you and Ron tryin' to be together and I ain't gon cause no problems. Ron and me are just cool. This somethin' that just happened. I thank I wanted to make a relationship wit Ron cause of the baby, but I know we ain't meant to be together. He really loves you though."

I didn't know what to say, "Yeah, I love him too."

"Well, I know ya'll gon be moving soon, Ron told me. I don't have no problem wit you. Me and my ex is suppose to be getting' us a place too. I just wanted to tell you that."

I thanked her for her comments and honesty. Ron got back on the phone.

"See you in a little while baby."

We hung up and I reflected on my conversation with Erica. She seemed to be understanding and okay with Ron and I being together instead of him being with her. Only time will tell if she is for real or faking.

Ron is coming over to my place for the first time. I think its time I tell him about my alternative lifestyle. We haven't had sex yet, but we've come close. I've been kind of holding back, because this time I want Ron to really work for me. I want him to show me he really wants me before I give in to having sex with him.

I'm not sure if I'm going to be able to give up sleeping with women totally. Mystery lady is always in my dreams, but I don't think I could whole heartedly commit to a woman. I like having a man around the house and even his masculine touch. It's nothing more comforting than being in a man's arms all night long.

I made Ron's favorite, lasagna with French bread. I even had a bottle of red wine and candles. I had dropped Simone off at Ms. Mary's so that we could be alone. I figured I'd put on something sexy, just in case. I chose a red slip dress and a pair of red lace thongs.

It was almost nine and he would be here in a minute. I was so nervous you would have thought it was my first time being with him.

The doorbell rang, and I took one last look at myself in the mirror. I answered the door and his eyes went from my head to my toes.

"Damn Lisa, you look good."

He walked in and hugged me so tight. He handed me a bag that had a bottle of Moet in it. I was impressed.

He looked around the living room and complimented my new place.

I wanted to give him the full tour, "Let me show you the rest of the place."

We walked through and he loved it. When we got to my bedroom, I showed him my whirlpool bathtub and he fell in love with it.

He hadn't seen my new bedroom set, but I could tell he was impressed. It was a four post bed with a canopy. I had sheer drapes hanging over the rails. The King size bed was enormous, but I promised myself a new bedroom set when I moved here.

The mood was so right. Besides, I'd had three glasses of wine before he got here and we were both sipping on one while we toured my home.

He finally broke the silence in my room, "Lisa, I had two shots of Patron before I left my house. I was trying to calm my nerves. I'm so nervous."

That was such a turn on. I walked over to him and kissed him. That felt electric.

"Ron, I have to tell you something before this night goes on."

He looked puzzled. I kissed him again, and he put his hands up my dress and caressed my ass. I was getting worked up, but I had to get this out before I gave into my desires.

"Ron, sit down."

He sat on the bed and I got on my knees between his legs.

"Ron, remember when we started having threesomes?"

His eyes were fixed on me, "Yes Lisa."

I held his hands and our eyes never left each other.

"If our relationship is going to work, I have to be honest with you. Ron, I like women. I like having sex with women."

He never took his eyes off me, "Lisa, I know you do. I hate that we ever did that a long time ago."

"Ron, I like women occasionally, but I don't want a relationship with one; at least not a committed one. I want us to be able to enjoy that together every once in a while."

He smiled, "You mean...we can be like swingers?"

I hadn't thought of it that way, "Yeah...I guess. I just want you to know before we take this thing to the next level. Can you accept that?"

He paused briefly. I knew he was in deep thought.

"Yes...yes Lisa, I can.

We kissed. The lasagna would have to wait. We had bigger fish to fry.

That night, we made love like we never have before. It was wonderful. I have missed the touch of a man and more importantly, the man I was once in love with.

I felt like I could be in love with him again. As we climaxed together I knew I was going to give it my all and he was going to do the same. A year ago, I never would have thought Ron and I would be working through our problems, but we were and I am so happy.

STACY

I can't wait to clock out today. Mitch has been on my nerves all day. Ever since I told him it was over he has really been a pain in my ass. He's got a gravy job so he can come to my job and hang out any time he wants. He is constantly in my face, and it's pissing me off.

His new little girlfriend kept giving me the evil eye. I guess she knows about me. Just as I was in my own zone, here he comes again.

"Hey baby girl. You want some lunch?"

Now he knows I haven't been accepting anything from him.

What I thought I Wanted

"No, I already have my lunch. I cooked last night and brought leftovers."

He had this stupid look on his face, "Oh, so you cooking now? I never got any home cooked meals. I guess Mike getting all that good stuff."

He eye balled me up and down, checking my body out.

"Mitch, look…we are at work and I don't want to go through this. You have a wife at home and a new little girlfriend running around here. I have a good man in my life. Let's just move on.

He was getting agitated, "Baby girl, I'm getting ready to separate from Jude. I talked to my daughters about it and everything."

I guess he thought that was what I wanted to hear. Maybe a year ago, but today I realize I don't want someone to leave who they're with for me. Especially when it's only because they find out someone else is in my life.

He was embarrassing me and making me upset. Two things I don't like to be at work.

"Mitch, I'm going to have to ask you to leave my job."

Just then, Mike walked up.

"Hey baby, you alright?"

He saw the look on my face and already knew the answer to his own question.

"Yeah, I'm fine," I lied.

The people that work around me were watching to see if it was going to be a fight. Mike looked at Mitch and handled himself like a true gentleman.

"Mitch, you doing alright?"

Mitch looked at Mike, "Yeah man, I'm alright. Just talking to 'our' girl here about a couple of thangs."

I know that 'our girl' comment didn't sit easy with Mike, but he kept his composure.

"Okay, well…I think we need to both get off her job before she gets in trouble. We don't want her to lose her job now do we?"

Mitch smirked, "If she did, she'll be alright."

Mitch patted his pants pocket where he keeps his money. He was being a real asshole. Mike didn't seem to think it was funny, at all.

"Mitch, let me holler at you for a minute. We'll see you later Stacy. I love you baby." I was so nervous I was almost scared to say I love you back. I thought about my Mother's advice.

I blew him a kiss and said, "I love you too baby."

Mitch and Mike walked away from my job talking and I wish I could have packed up my things and left work for the day. I wondered what the out come of their talk would be.

I was taking my last break of the day when Kim came over to me and told me how everybody was talking about Mitch and Mike on my job. I gave her the details of what had happened.

I had been trying to call Mike on his cell phone, but I couldn't get in touch with him. I was starting to get worried. I asked Kim had she seen either Mike or Mitch. She hadn't seen them either.

I called Lisa on her cell, and asked her had she seen them. She told me the same story. She heard about Mike and Mitch on my job, but she hadn't seen them.

"Damn, this is crazy" she thought to herself. The rest of the day took forever to end. My girls and I were talking, waiting for the clock to strike three so we could punch out when Mike came up behind me, and grabbed me around my waist.

"Hey baby!"

I spun around, "Where you been? I've been calling your cell all day."

He didn't crack a smile.

167

"I was talking to Mitch for quite some time and I had some thinking to do. I need to talk to you."

I was nervous. I wondered what Mitch told him. Whatever Mike wanted to talk about, I was ready. I wasn't going to let Mitch ruin my relationship.

I asked him, "You want to talk now?"

He nodded yes.

"Okay, I'll meet you at your house."

We punched out and I told the girls I would be at Mike's house. As I got in my car, my cell phone rang. It was Mitch. I wanted so desperately to know what they talked about so I answered.

"Hey baby girl, I see your man really cares about you."

"You think so?"

I couldn't help but be sarcastic for a stupid comment like that. He waited for me to explode, but I didn't.

"So I guess it's over for us. He said ya'll are serious."

I finally broke it down for Mitch one more time, "We are serious Mitch. Why are you giving me such a hard time about my relationship? It's not like you don't have anyone else. You know we were never going to really be together or get married, or even have a family for that matter. The times I was pregnant, you didn't even want the baby. Why are you trying to act so brand new now?"

"Maybe because I didn't know what I had in you. I'm an old man and should've been much wiser about things. Jude and I been married all these years and I never saw the bad stuff in our relationship because I always had someone else to make up the parts that was missin. Now that I see it, I don't want to lose it. I'm just about ready to do what it takes to make you mine."

He launched that last comment with a twist of anger. I was approaching Mike's street and was more than ready to end the conversation.

"Well Mitch, I'm sorry you realize it now, but sometimes we realize things a little too late. I have to go."

Without another word, Mitch hung up the phone.

I unlocked the door to Mike's house and felt a bit awkward. I've been staying with him almost every day now. A lot of my clothes were there and I had even been cooking, washing and grocery shopping.

I sat on the sofa in the living room. He was already sitting in the matching chair.

I jumped right in to it, "What's the matter, baby?"

He looked at me with tears in his eyes, "Did you go over to Mitch's house recently?"

My heart fell to my shoes. I didn't want to lie.

"Yes, I did...but it wasn't for what you think."

The tears he'd probably held back all day started to fall from his eyes.

"Why Stacy?"

I was so hurt because I knew I was the cause of those tears.

"I went over there to tell him I couldn't see him anymore."

He put his head down, "Mitch told me the only reason you two didn't sleep together was because his wife came home. Is that true?"

I shook my head, "No, I went over there and we did eat together. He thought I was going to sleep with him because I went upstairs, but I never took a stitch of my clothes off. I was waiting for him to come upstairs so I could tell him."

The tears from my man's eyes continued to fall.

"So you did go to their bedroom?"

"Yes, I did...maybe I shouldn't have, but I didn't know really how to tell him I wasn't going to see him anymore."

"So his wife came home?"

"Yes, she did and I went out the balcony doors, got in my car and drove away. I left my purse and he met me at a hotel to give it to me. I know he thought I was going to sleep with him, but I didn't. I got my purse and told him it was over. Did he tell you that?"

He nodded his head, "Yeah he told me about the purse and the hotel, except his ending was way different."

I started to cry because Mitch was trying to destroy my relationship with Mike.

"I love you, Mike. I haven't slept with anyone else since we've been together. I love my life with you and I want to be with you."

I had never spoken with such desperation for any man before Mike. Right then, I knew he was the one. I was convinced to do whatever it took to keep him.

Mike put his head in his hands and took a deep breath. Raising his head again, he locked eyes with mine. All I could see was hurt and pain shooting directly at me.

"I followed you to the Residence Inn, and with my own eyes, saw you go in."

"I went in, but I didn't sleep with him. He wouldn't give me my purse unless I went in and talked to him."

"Mitch told me you would be at his house that day. He told me he could still hit it if he wanted to. I didn't believe him, that's why he told me to see for myself."

I couldn't believe what I was hearing, but I had a surprise for Mike.

"You know, I have something I want you to hear. I've always taped my heated conversations with Mitch in case I ever needed to use them against him."

I went to my purse, pulled out my cell phone and let Mike listen to the conversation Mitch and I had after I left my purse. He sat there quietly and listened to the message. Then I played the message from today. His eyes began to dry up and I could see relief on his face. After the messages were done playing, I looked at him with sincerity.

He came over to me, "Baby, you don't know how glad I am that you had those messages. Mitch had painted me a horrible picture of you. I thank God you are so smart."

For the first time all day, he smiled. I was happy too, because I had proven myself to the man I love. We kissed and made love.

Make up sex is the best sex to have. A couple having all those mixed emotions being released is priceless. It's beautiful and it's a bond that only the two of them share. No one can break that bond. It's like we had become one.

AMBER

I thoroughly enjoyed myself at Lisa's spot. I even got tested and paid my membership. She and Ron seem to be doing pretty good. We all went to the club the other night and had a ball.

Lisa and Ron hooked up with that lady Lisa always ends up with and I saw Carrington. It hasn't been so bad without Ameri lately, I guess because I have Carrington.

We went out for lunch and had a good time. No sex that day, just a nice lunch with light conversation. Turns out Carrington is a business owner and has a twin sister. He doesn't have any children and is thirty-two. He's ready to be in a committed relationship, get married and start a family. I felt him on that.

We have been talking a lot, but I'm kind of reluctant to see him too much because of Ameri.

Ameri hasn't been completely cut off. He's was on his way to my house, and that kind of excited me. We haven't been together in a minute because of all the time he spends working and watching the kids.

I think I'm getting tired of the whole married man thing. I don't even talk about the divorce with him anymore. I noticed that he doesn't bring it up either. I'm sure he's happy about that.

The gatehouse just called, Ameri is on his way to my door. I checked myself one more time in the mirror. I smiled at the body hugging long black dress I had on in the full length mirror.

The door bell rings, "Just a minute!"

I opened the door and there he was, looking magnificent. "Hey baby!" he said in that deep baritone voice.

We hugged and he smelled so good. I didn't want to let go. He sat on the sofa and quickly removed his cell phone from his pocket and turned it to silent. He probably didn't want it to disturb us.

I offered him and drink and he gladly accepted.

"Yeah, make me one of those purple passion drinks. That drink is the bomb."

I smiled because I knew they were.

We sat on the sofa and watched "Stepmom", with Julia Roberts and Susan Sarandon. I'm an emotional person and cried when the two women talked about the daughter's wedding day. Ameri could tell I was crying and kissed me on my head.

He spoke softly, "My wife has cancer, but it's in remission now. You think you could do what Julia Robert's is doing?"

I was shocked to hear him say that. Not because of the question he asked me, but because I remembered his wife telling me that he told the other women in the past that she does, and how that was a lie. I was heated, but kept my cool…for the moment.

"Of course baby, I wouldn't have it any other way. I would be there for you and your kids."

I was messed up and couldn't even keep my mind on the movie anymore. I decided to probe a little further. I couldn't lay my head on his chest any longer.

I sat up and looked at him, "How long has she been in remission?"

He kept his eyes on the movie, "For about two years now, but she has an appointment with her specialist because she thinks something is wrong. That's why I haven't been around much. She's been real sick and needed extra help with the kids."

He looked at me, "I knew I hadn't spent anytime with you so I had to put my foot down and tell her I had something else to do. I couldn't keep neglecting my baby."

I looked on in disbelief. I wasn't sure what to believe.

After the movie went off, I made Ameri some lunch and he asked what I was doing later.

Even though he had his cell phone on silent, he still checked it every fifteen minutes. I could tell he was getting calls from her. I told him I was going out with Lisa. He had the nerve to get pissed.

"You sure you going out with Lisa, or do you have a new man in your life?"

I smacked my lips, "Ameri, you got room to be questioning me? You're married and although you two are 'supposed' to be going through a divorce, you spend most of your time at her house."

He was mad, but I didn't care. He finally responded to what I said.

"Look Amber, you know my situation is delicate. I just told you my wife may be having a relapse and all you can do is think of yourself."

I couldn't believe his ass, here I am sitting at home on a Saturday waiting for his ass to drop by when I could be out shopping with my girls, getting my hair done or a pedicure.

Instead when his tired ass said he was coming, I cancelled my hair appointment and pedicure to see him. I was ready for his ass to go.

"Look Ameri, I don't want to argue with you. There is nothing to argue about. I'm going out tonight and you'll be watching the kids. I don't see the problem."

He looked at me, "Yeah, okay...you don't see the problem. I don't like you hanging out at bars with your girl."

"Well Ameri, I don't like a lot of things, but I can't change them. We can't always have what we want, now can we? Besides, your wife is calling you. You keep looking at your phone, just answer it!"

He huffed, and answered his phone, "Hello!"

I could tell it was a woman's voice on the other end.

"Okay, alright, bye!"

He looked at me, "I'm out of here."

I opened the door for him, "Bye!"

July shutdown was coming up and Stacy, Kim, Lisa and I were going to the Kohler Spa in Wisconsin for a Girlfriends getaway. We had been planning it for over six months. I couldn't wait for our trip.

Lisa and I talked about how cool it was going to be as we were on our way to the spot.

"Yeah, but my birthday will be here in a couple of weeks. We hanging out downtown again?"

She never took her eyes off the road, "Hell naw! Last time we went to Belle Isle you met Mr. Ameri who turned out to be a real loser."

We both started laughing. Lisa stopped laughing long enough to say, "We got your birthday all planned out. Not like you guys did on my mine. We aren't going to a strip club."

We laughed again. We got there about ten o'clock and the lot was full tonight. We did our usual and were looking sexier than hell when we approached the bar.

The guy behind the bar knew us, "Hey Bruno, give us the usual."

Bruno had learned to make our drinks to the tee. I spotted Carrington and Lisa was waiting on the mystery lady she affectionately called Ann. I walked over to talk to Carrington.

"Hey, good looking."

He smiled, "I should be saying that to you. I was hoping you would be here tonight."

I blushed, "You came here waiting to see if I'd show up?"

He smiled and laughed, "Not exactly. I told you I'm a business man with my own business."

I didn't understand, "Yeah…so what does that have to do with you being here."

He smiled, "This is my business."

I was shocked, "You own this place?"

He nodded, "Yes, but not many people know I'm the owner. Let's go to my office and talk."

I followed him speechlessly to a huge office with mahogany furniture and a fireplace that made the office so cozy.

"Carrington, I wouldn't have ever guessed that you owned this place."

He looked at me as he sat down behind his desk to turn on all the monitors that watched every inch of his building.

"I like it that people think I'm just another patron of this establishment."

I walked over to him and sat in his lap. As we looked onto the monitors, I saw Ann walk in and Lisa's face lit up.

"My girl is crazy about Ann."

He looked at Ann, "Yeah, she's been a member for a long time. Nice lady, just been in a bad relationship. Many people come here to get away from real life. That's why I created this place; a place where you can escape without leaving the state. My place gives you a couple of ours of fantasy every night. I just wish I had someone to share my life with."

He gazed into my eyes and we kissed.

"Amber, I would love to make love to you right now, but I don't want you to think that's all I want. I want to date you and get to know you. I want to see where we can go with this."

My heart fluttered with joy.

"I would like that too."

Chapter 13

KIM

Life hasn't been too bad lately. I've been looking over my shoulder, because I don't know when Joseph is going to make his move.

Malcolm has been my main concern. I know the detectives have been watching him closely, because Joseph may try and go for him first.

I haven't checked my post office box in weeks. I guess I've been scared. I decided today that I would check it. I've been contemplating it all day at work. I made up my mind to pick up my mail before I picked up some sandwiches from Star Deli.

I held my breath as I opened the little door with my key to my post office box. The usual bills were in there with an unusual letter. It had no return address on it. Looking at the handwriting, I knew it was from Joseph.

I immediately called Agent Matthews and he agreed to meet me at the house. I picked up three corned beef specials and went home.

I sat down at my kitchen table and opened the letter,

"Dear Kim, I didn't think you would go so far as to feature me on America's Most Wanted. I was shocked. I figured you would just run to another state. Now you got my picture on the ten most wanted list. I can't believe you. I saw my picture plastered on a billboard sign on I-75 as one of Michigan's Most Wanted.

I guess you meant what you said on t.v., you're not running anymore. I see your man isn't running either. How is my son doing? He looks a lot like me doesn't he? I bet it's not a day that goes by that you don't look at him and see me. Are you scared he may act like me?

I never meant to hurt you Kim, but you made me anger. You were trying to leave me and I couldn't have that. That noisy ass neighbor should have minded her own business. I hate things are going to have to end like this Kim. I have enough money for us to live a good life forever.

My mother told me the police are on her heels. You wrong for bringing the law to my Mom. With all this publicity, I guess I'm going to have to hurry up and do what I got to do and move on. Can't wait to see you Kim. Can't wait to feel me inside of you, right before I end it all!

Hugs and Kisses, Joseph."

He's lost his mind. Before I would let him have sex with me, I'd kill myself first.

Agent Matthews looked at the envelope and saw the post mark was from that post office. He called the post office and asked for the security camera footage to be pulled. He took the letter and was out the door.

Alan, Malcolm and I ate our sandwiches and we talked about the letter. We were becoming a regular family, besides the crazy lunatic that was stalking us.

After we ate, Malcolm went to his room to do homework. Alan and I got ready for bed. We showered together and held each other so close. After our shower, we lay in the bed naked and watching the news.

It's so many crimes going on. Family killing family, I never thought I may make headline news one day very soon.

Alan turned over towards me, "Baby, I have something very important to ask you and I feel it can't wait."

"What is it Alan?"

He caressed my face, "I know you have Ms. Mary and she is a great person, but she is older."

I nodded my head, "Yes she is."

"Well, I'm not saying Joseph is going to harm you, but we have to talk about this, but if he does, I want to take care of Malcolm."

I started to cry, "Are you serious?"

A single tear rolled down his cheek, "Yes, I love him baby. He is a good kid and I only want the best for him."

I didn't know what to say. He got up from the bed and went to the dresser.

He got back in the bed, "Which brings me to my question...."

He didn't have to ask me if I was okay with that because I knew if something happened to me, Ms. Mary was too old to keep Malcolm.

I thought about asking Lisa or Amber, but I think Alan would be what's best for him.

Alan then cleared his voice, "I talked to Malcolm about this already and he was okay with it. Now, Kim would you marry me?"

OH MY GOD! He just asked me to marry him. He talked to Malcolm already. He flashed me a two carat solitaire ring. I was so excited.

"YES! Yes a thousand times! You have made me so happy in such a short period of time. I can't believe this. In all that I am going through, you want to marry me!"

He took the ring out the box and slid it onto my finger.

"Kim, a man knows what he wants and it doesn't take years to figure it out. I knew you were something special the first time I laid eyes on you at the gym. I don't care what your name used to be, what it is now, or what it may have to change to in the future. I'm in love with the woman lying here beside me. I love her and her son, who I consider my son. We will make it through this. I have already made us reservations in the Poconos during your two week shut-down and we will be married in less than two months. There is no use in waiting."

Alan and I enjoyed the rest of the weekend as a couple. We went to the movies, watched old movies at home, bowling, and plenty of sex. As the weekend ended, I couldn't wait for Amber's get together next weekend.

Since I was going to be hanging with the girls the weekend of Amber's birthday, I decided to announce my engagement then. Amber's birthday fell on a Thursday, a work day. So, the rest of the girls and I decided to bring in food to celebrate. We always did that for each of our birthdays.

During our lunch, we laughed and joked. We were given forty-five minutes for lunch and we made the best of every minute.

Mitch walked passed the break room and waved at Stacy. She waved back, but you could tell she was annoyed. All of us were so happy.

I brought my camera and took pictures. After our break, it was back to work. As I approached my job, the Supervisor came up to me.

"You have an emergency phone call up front."

I ran up the aisle towards the front. By the time I got to the phone, I was out of breath.

"Hello!"

"Well, you got to the phone pretty fast."

I recognized the voice immediately, it was Joseph. I grabbed a pen off the desk and wrote a note to my supervisor. He nodded and took off.

"What do you want?" I said with as much attitude as I could muster up.

"Now is that any way to treat the father of your child, the man you almost married?"

I was scared, but stood my ground, "Key word being almost Joseph. That means didn't quite make it."

He got angry and started yelling, "I will always be Malcolm's father. You hear me! You are pissing me off Kim!"

181

He quickly calmed down, "Look, I didn't call you for this. How is your day going?"

I couldn't believe this "Jekel & Hyde" personality.

"My day is going wonderful. And yours?"

"Mine was going alright until I came back to my hotel room to find the FBI at the hotel. I guess I'm not as slick as I thought. Lucky I keep all my important stuff on me."

My supervisor came back to the desk and nodded yes to me.

"Is that all you called me for Joseph? To tell me the FBI was in your hotel room?"

He laughed, "No, I called to tell you Malcolm gets out of school at 2:30 pm and I will be there to pick him up!"

He hung up. I dropped the phone and screamed.

STACY

After Amber's lunch celebration, we all returned to our jobs. Mitch was really starting to creep me out. Luckily we all took the CCW class together. By all of us being single women, Lisa thought it was a good thing for us, and registered all of us for the class. We even went together and bought our guns.

We were supposed to go to the gun range once a week. I'm not saying I will have to shoot Mitch, but at least I have some form of protection.

He still comes by my job. I guess he thought he broke Mike and I up, but nothing has changed. In fact Mitch's little fiasco only made us stronger. Speaking of, here comes my baby. He looks so good in his coveralls.

"Hey sexy," I said, giving him a sexy smile.

"Hey baby, you alright."

"Yeah, why you ask me that?"

"I saw Mitch coming up the aisle, but when he saw me, he turned the other way. I thought he may have come down here."

I thought about it, "Naw, he came pass the break room while we were eating with Amber. He just waved and kept going. I don't think he means any harm. I just think he is sucker stroking now. He tried to break us up and it didn't work."

He looked at me like I was naïve.

"Yeah, well I hope I don't have to fuck Mitch's old ass up."

I came off my platform and hugged him, "Baby, don't worry about nothing. We are together and he knows my heart is with you."

He smiled, "Okay baby, I'll see you at home after I get my hair cut."

I smiled at him, he was calling his home ours, "Okay see you at home."

I got off work and headed to the grocery store. I stopped by my mother's house first.

"Hey Mom."

She smiled at me, "Hey stranger. Where you been?"

I looked at her with my head cocked to the side, "You know where I been, over Mike's house."

She smiled, "Oh, when you two just gonna go ahead and tie the knot. He is a wonderful man. You know he came by the other day and put up my new ceiling fan for me."

"Yeah, I know Ma, he told me. You think we make a good couple?"

She laughed, "Girl, you two are great together. I see a lot of changes in you since you been with him. You dropped all them zeros and got yourself a real man."

I smiled, she was right. I haven't had the desire to be with anyone else.

183

"I don't know Ma. We are taking it one day at a time. I don't know if he wants to marry me. I think he's just trying to get pass my past."

She lit a cigarette, "I think he is way past that. Do you think you could spend the rest of your life with him?"

I thought about it, without much hesitation, "Yeah, Mom, I could. The thing is sometimes feel like I could never be good enough for Mike, at least not good enough to be his wife. Ma, what if I'm not good enough?"

She looked at me with a quizzical look, "What do you mean, not good enough?"

"Ma, you know we talk about everything. You know I don't have the best track record at the plant."

She smirked, "Yeah, you was all about making them dollars to shop. Now you realize the Gucci, Dolce and Gabana, and Fendi don't mean anything at the end of the day. Baby, you've grown up. You changed your whole out look on life. Mike and I talked about you the other day, we admire your attitude and how you don't care what anybody thinks. You stand your ground and won't lie to save yourself."

I thought for a moment, "Ma, you know I always felt like as long as I was making plenty of money, I had everything. You're right I do realize that money isn't everything. I started having feelings for Mitch and I didn't want to accept it. I wanted to be with Mitch. I wanted to be his wife, and the money didn't matter anymore. He just didn't want me."

My mother looked so sad, "Baby, Mitch is an old player. He was never going to leave his wife. Men like him keep their wives and keep their women too. I told you, I've been there. I'm glad you woke up at an earlier age than me. Now you have a chance to be in a relationship where you two can do whatever you want, whenever you want. Don't mess it up for nobody or nothing."

I loved when my Mother and I talked like that. We hugged and told each other we loved one another.

"Well, I got to get home Ma. I'm cooking steak and rice tonight."

She laughed, "See what I mean, my baby has grown up."

I stopped at the grocery store on my way 'home' and picked up a few items. I was walking towards the car looking for my keys when I saw him.

"Mitch, what are you doing here?"

He smiled, "Hey baby girl, I was picking up a couple of things for a friend of mine."

Typical Mitch, he's probably cooking over some little girls house.

"Oh, that's cool. You been okay?"

He smiled, "Yeah, baby I been awright. Just gettin' used to not being wit you."

He always makes me uncomfortable with that kind of talk.

"Well, I got to go. I got to get home to cook dinner."

He smiled, "Oh you cooking tonight too?"

I smiled, "Yeah, see you at work Mitch."

I put my groceries in the car and got out of there. He just stood there and watched me leave. He was really creeping me out. I got home in no time flat and started making dinner.

My cell phone started ringing, it was Mitch. I didn't answer. I don't want to talk about him. I wouldn't have ever guessed he would be so messed up behind our break up. I guess maybe he did care more than I thought he did.

I turned my cell phone off and put it in my purse. Anyone who needed to talk to me had Mike's home number. The house phone rang. I looked at the caller ID, it was Mike.

"Hey baby," he was laughing. "Baby, your ex-man is funny as hell."

I was puzzled, "Why you say that? What did he do?"

185

"You remember Danetta?"

How could I forget who Danetta was? She was Mike's ex-girlfriend.

"Yeah Mike. What about her?"

"She called me today and told me Mitch asked her why we broke up. She was paying back some money she owed him and he asked a lot of questions about her and I."

That was weird, "What did she say?"

"She told him, that we were better as friends. That it wasn't any hard feelings between us and she was happy for me and you."

Well, that was cool. I still don't know why Mike got such a big kick out of that.

"That was it?"

He laughed, "Naw. She said Mitch told her she didn't have to pay the money back if she could work on getting me away from you."

I couldn't believe Mitch's ass, "Are you serious? What the hell is going on with Mitch?"

He laughed, "I don't know, but evidently he is missing what he had. I'll see you in a minute baby. I just had to call you and tell you that."

I hung up the phone and pondered over what Mike just told me. I don't know what is going on with Mitch, but I hope he gets it together. I guess at this point, all I can do is say a prayer for him because I'm not going backwards.

LISA

Ron and I have been spending the night over each others house. Simone is loving it. She has two bedrooms. One decorated in Dora and the other decorated in Princess.

We finally got LaRon's room together at Ron's house. We made it adorable. LaRon looks just like Ron.

Since Ron has been working steadily, he gives me money every week. I finally met Erica. She is a plus size girl. Mocha skin and very shapely. She looks to be about 5' 3." I can see why Ron liked her. You can't really tell she is straight hood until she starts to talk.

We went over to his Mother's house to pick the baby up. Simone adores her baby brother. She always wants to kiss him. She has been fussing at Ron, because she wants him to keep LaRon for the weekend. After we both got off work, we went to go get him. We were going to pick Simone up next.

Soon as we pulled up, Erica came storming out of his Mother's house. She had on some daisy duke shorts and a halter top, with her hair all over her head. She walked right past Ron and straight to me.

"Did Ron tell you we slept together?"

I was not expecting this, "No, Ron hasn't said anything like that to me."

He ran over to the side of the car we were on.

"Erica, stop lying! Why you doing this?"

She rolled her eyes at Ron, "I'm sick of you lyin' to me and her! You ain't never stop bein' in my face. You was suppose to be helpin' me to go back to school and get my GED and you ain't did nothin' but try to get in my panties!"

I didn't know what to do. All I know is the way she came on me, I had to be ready. If this bitch swings, it's on.

"Look Erica, I don't know anything about none of this. Ron are you fucking her?"

He looked at me, "Hell nah! Baby, I don't want this girl. She just trippin' cause she been asking me about us getting back together and raising LaRon and her other two kids."

I was shocked. I didn't know the girl had two more kids.

She started yelling, "Ask his Mama!"

Ms. Gladys was standing in the door. I turned my focus to her.

"Lisa, baby, you know how a man is. I was in my room and I heard that girl pushing for sex with Ron. He kept sayin' no, but she kept on pushing. She told him if he didn't have sex with her, he couldn't see his son. Now, I don't know if anything happened cause I left the house for bingo."

Ron started talking, "Erica you full of shit! All my Momma said is true. I didn't sleep with her. I told her to get the fuck out my Momma's house with that mess. I haven't been seeing him because she wants sex and money in exchange for me seeing my son."

"Erica, you trying to force Ron to sleep with you?"

She looked all crazy, "I don't have to force no man to want this!" She rubbed all over her body, "Ron miss this pussy and be tryin' to get some of it. "

I was tired of listening to her shit, "Look, are you going to let him pick up LaRon or not?"

She smacked her lips, "Nah, I don't want my baby somewhere I can't come. I don't know where Ron lives at now."

Ron had baby mama drama going on for real.

I looked at Ron, "Okay, Ron let's go."

We got ready to get in the car and she charged at me, "Bitch, you the reason why we can't be together. You and your bitch ass daughter."

I got so mad, I cocked the hoe in her face and laid her out on the grass.

I stood over her ass, "No one talks about mine. You got that? Now, when you want to be civilized, give us a call. Let's go Ron."

She was screaming, "I'm going to kill your ass bitch. Ron is my man and I ain't letting him go. You a dead bitch."

Ron pulled off and then stopped. I knew he wanted to get out and whup her ass

"Ron it ain't worth it. Let's go."

He looked at me, "You right!"

We turned the corner and didn't look back. We were out of there.

Once we picked Simone up, we went to my house. We ate Pizza Hut and Simone went to her room to play.

"Lisa, I'm sorry I didn't tell you about how Erica been trying to get me to have sex with her."

I wasn't mad about that, "That's alright Ron. I knew she wasn't over you."

He looked disgusted, "Yeah, I thought she was straight, but the other guy went to jail so now she wants to make it work with me. All she does now is get drunk and talk about hurting you and Simone."

I was mad about that, "Now Ron. That was one thing you should have told me about. You never know how crazy a woman can be. Does she have a car?"

"Yeah an old Chevy Caprice."

"What color is it?"

"It's blue. Why you asking me these questions?"

"Ron, I just bust this girl in her face and she has already told you me and Simone is the reason you two can't be together. I got to be on the look out for her. Don't you agree?"

He thought about it, "Yeah, you right because Erica will do just about anything. I mean she has robbed dudes before and she told me how she shot at her other baby daddy. She ain't afraid of going to jail."

I sat at the kitchen table and thought about this whole situation. Man, Ron and I finally get it together and now we got the psycho baby mama running the streets of Detroit. I guess I'm gonna have to bring back the old Lisa and get ghetto with this bitch.

What I thought I Wanted

KIM

The FBI got me to the school in no time flat. The Southfield Police had already gotten to the school. I jumped out the car and ran toward the building, I was frantic. I wanted to be sure that Malcolm was okay.

The FBI agents were running behind me. As I entered the school, police were everywhere.

One officer grabbed me, "Ma'am you can't go in there."

I started screaming, "Where is my son? Where is Malcolm?"

As I was trying to break loose from the officer's grasp, Agent Matthews was approaching.

"Officer! Let her go. She is the parent!"

The Officer released me from his grasp, "I'm sorry Ma'am."

I ran to Agent Matthews, "Where is my son!?"

He held my arms, "He's okay. We got to him just in time. He is a little shaken up, but he is going to be alright. I need you to calm down, for Malcolm's sake."

I understood what Agent Matthews was saying, but I needed to see my son.

"I need to see him, please. I have to see that he is alright."

I was crying hysterically.

Agent Matthews continued to remain calm, "Kim, the other agents are questioning Malcolm. We have to try and get the information while it's fresh on Malcolm's mind."

Agent Matthews ushered me off to a small office to speak with me further.

"We don't want to make life at this school hard for Malcolm to continue or break your cover. We have talked with the Principal and all the students are being let out. We have to protect you and Malcolm."

"Is he alright! Did Joseph hurt him?"

Agent Matthews looked at me, "We'll get into all that in a moment. I'll be right back."

I felt like I was in this room for hours before Agent Matthews returned. I was so shaken up I couldn't sit still.

He came back with a photo, "Is this Joseph?"

I looked at the picture and covered my mouth in fright. It looked like him, but a bit older that I remembered. He had altered his appearance. He'd grown a mustache and a full beard. It seemed he had shaven his head bald and looked to have had some sort of cosmetic surgery. His cheek bones were a little broader and his lips were a little fuller, but I knew those eyes. Those eyes were like death staring back at me.

"Yes, it's Joseph," I cried. "Is he still here? Is he still in the building?"

Agent Matthews looked at me, "No! He has been rushed to Providence Hospital."

I got upset all over again, if Joseph was at the hospital then what had happened to my son?

"Agent Matthews, please let me see my son!"

He looked at me, "Follow me."

We went down a corridor and into another office. Malcolm was sitting at a desk while a lady seemed to write down everything he was saying.

I ran to him, "Malcolm!"

He turned and saw me, "Mom!"

I held my baby so tight. As I pushed him back to look at him, I realized he was covered in blood.

"What happened?"

His eyes welled up with tears, "Mom, I…I…."

I looked at him, "What baby?"

Agent Matthews told Malcolm he would explain everything to me. He instructed Malcolm to continue to speak with the Detective sitting at the desk. Malcolm nodded his head and returned to the desk. I didn't want to leave him but Agent

Matthews led me back to the office where I slumped down in the chair.

"I can't take this. What happened?"

"Let me go get you some water. This is going to be a long story."

For the next hour, Agent Matthews explained that Joseph had been working right here at the school. He was working as the assistant coach on the football team. He was using the alias name of Juan Santiago. By Joseph being fair skinned and having wavy hair, he was passing for a mixed Hispanic/African-American man.

He had been working for the school for the last nine months. He had created a completely new background and identity.

By him being a quarterback in high school, Joseph loved football and always stayed active in sports. It really wasn't surprising he was working as a coach, but I didn't expect he would be working in my son's school and talking to my son everyday.

Agent Matthews told me, Joseph approached Malcolm as he was leaving school and told him he would give him a ride home. Joseph told Malcolm he wanted to discuss some plays with him.

Agent Matthews kind of laughed as he told his story, "Your son is a good judge of character. He told me he felt something odd and uncomfortable about Coach Santiago today, especially when the Coach said he talked to you about taking him home. He said it was the look in his eyes."

I knew the look. Agent Matthews continued, "Since Malcolm ends his day in gym, he and Joseph were going to walk out together. While they were still in the gym, Joseph started asking Malcolm about his father."

I covered my mouth, just then Malcolm came into the office. He looked at Agent Matthews.

"Did you tell her?"

"I was in the middle of telling her, but you can finish. I had just got to Joseph asking you about your dad."

Malcolm sat down and held my hand, "Mom, he started talking about how proud my dad must be and how he would like to meet my father. I was starting to feel funny about all the things he was saying and how he was pushing to find out information about my father. I decided to see where he was coming from, and thought this may be my Dad I'm talking to."

I told him, "My father left me when I was little."

Malcolm's eyes widened, "He got mad. He said 'I don't believe your Father left you'. The usual accent he has was leaving fast, and I looked around the locker room and no one was there with us. I reached into my locker and got my backpack and we started walking toward the exit doors. He told me it must be hard not having a father figure. I knew if this man was my father this would get him. I told him I have a great step-father. He helps me practice, takes me to Detroit Lions games, helps with my homework and even talks to me about girls. I think he is great."

He leaned in and said, "To put the nail in the coffin, I told him my step-dad told me he would never leave me. That was it, Joseph grabbed me and threw me against the lockers. He started yelling, 'No one can take your Daddy's place.' I knew it was him."

I started to cry and my son wiped my tears.

"Baby, I'm sorry you had to go through this."

He looked at Agent Matthews who nodded and looked back at me.

"Mom there is more...we started to fight in the locker room. He pulled out a knife and tried to stab me. He told me he was going to finish what he started. We started fighting. I knocked the knife out his hand and he tried to scramble to pick it back up."

I looked at my son's lip and face, he was bruised up.

He continued, "I reached for my backpack and pulled out your gun Mom. I had been carrying it for the last two days because I just felt something was going to happen. He got up and ran at me with the knife, and I shot him."

My hand went over my mouth and all I could say was, "Oh my God."

Malcolm started to cry, "He dropped the knife and kept coming toward me. He grabbed onto me and we fell. He fell on top of me. I pushed him off of me and ran back into the gym where my coach was. I told him to call the police and collapsed onto the gym floor."

Agent Matthews told me Joseph is in critical condition and was requesting to see me. I was so happy my son survived this attack. I wanted to confront my child's father and told Agent Matthews, "There is nothing more I would like than to see Joseph McAfee."

I got to the hospital, escorted by FBI. Once we got to the room Joseph was occupying, there were police standing outside his room. Agent Matthews, Alan and Malcolm were there. They all asked me if I needed them to go in with me.

It had been twenty-four hours since the incident that left my son alive and his father clinging to life. I'm glad it came out this way, because I would have hated to see me son in the hospital because of his father.

It was three thirty in the afternoon, and Lisa, Stacy, and Amber were getting off the elevator just as I was getting my nerve up to face what I had been running from for years.

It was Friday, Malcolm and I didn't go to school or work. We spent the morning thanking God for his mercy and appreciating each other. Alan was so happy this nightmare was finally over and the predator had been captured.

Lisa, Stacy and Amber hugged me. They too asked if I wanted them to go in with me.

I told them "No this is something I have to do for myself."

Agent Matthews told me he had to go in with me, but he would stand back as Joseph and I talked. I nodded. I took a deep breath and entered the hospital room with Agent Matthews behind.

As I walked toward the bed, I saw they had handcuffed Joseph to the rails of the bed. I reached the bed to view a man's face I once loved. Agent Matthews approached the bed. Joseph's eyes were closed.

Agent Matthews spoke, "Joseph McAfee?"

Joseph's eyes opened, "Yes."

"I am Agent Matthews, you wanted to see Kim and she agreed to see you. I have to lay some ground rules for you. If you try any foolishness or try and upset Ms. Mitchell, this meeting will be over. The next time you will see her is in a court room, understood?"

He nodded slowly. Agent Matthew moved back and I remained at Joseph's beside.

"You raised a pretty strong son."

I looked at him sternly, "Yes, I did. Why did you come back? Why couldn't you just have left us alone?"

He cleared his throat, "Because you were my family and you left me."

I gritted my teeth, "You tried to kill me! What the hell did you expect?"

He talked with a raspy voice, "I expected you to work it out with me. I couldn't find you for years. Finally, I got a lead from my mother. She had friends in Michigan who knew Ms. Mary and that's how I found out you were in Michigan. I got the job at the school to watch my son."

I fought back the tears, "Well, I'm glad you are finally in custody. No more running for me and for MY SON."

He looked at me with those cold eyes, "He's my son too."

195

I smirked, "No he's not. You gave him up when you tried to kill us."

He cleared his throat again, "I still love you Kim."

I looked at him with disgust, "How can you love me and try to end my life? Please! I got a new life now, great friends and a wonderful relationship."

He closed his eyes as if what I said made him feel pain. He opened them and stared into my eyes with hatred.

"Yeah, Alan seems to be a nice man. I've gone to the gym and had a couple of sessions with him. He can't take my place. I'm still Malcolm's father. My blood runs through his body."

I got strong and looked that miserable man in his eyes.

"I hope you rot in jail, that you never see the light of day again. It's over now and I have nothing else to say to you. In less than two months, I'll be married and in less than six, I will be graduating from college as a Registered Nurse. You didn't stop me. My son and I survived all your bullshit. Goodbye Joseph McAfee and good riddance."

I turned to walk out.

He called my name, "Kim!...Kim!...Kim!"

I walked out the room and everyone was waiting for my response. I smiled at my friends, my family, my loved ones.

"Let's celebrate, the birthday of Amber and the death of my past!"

We all yelled and cheered as we headed for the elevators.

E'nise

Chapter 14

AMBER

A year has gone by and I'm a year older. My girls are still here for me and we are headed to Fishbones again. I love that place. The Alligator Voodoo is the bomb!

Usually we all ride together, but this year we are meeting up at the restaurant. I haven't heard from Ameri since he called me for my birthday. I guess it was nice he came by on my birthday and bought me this gorgeous diamond heart pendant and chain. It looks good on me.

Carrington has been calling me and taking me out. I just don't miss Ameri like I used to.

Thanks to my girl Stacy, she is making me realize nothing good comes from a relationship with a married man. They promise you the world and never deliver.

She told me, "Sure they give you some happiness, about two hours worth and then they have to go back to resume their normal lives."

She was so right. I thought back to the times Ameri and I spent together. They were nice, but always cut short or ended with him leaving before I was ready for him to go. I thought my situation was different, because he was going through a divorce. After sitting down with Stacy, I realized my situation was similar to hers and even Havana, my old co-worker.

It's hard to break away from someone when you have fallen in love with them. Even when you know deep down, nothing good is ever going to come from the relationship. A woman still has hope for her feelings. I guess that's where I am.

I feel so bad about passing judgment on Stacy and Havana. You never know what situation you will find yourself in. I've learned never to judge anyone, because you never know what you may have to come to.

My grandmother taught me that saying as a little girl and now at thirty-one years old, I finally understand the true meaning.

On my birthdays I always like to think back on the last past year of my life and see what I accomplished and what I've learned. This last year I learned how wise my grandmother was and not to be so quick to judge anymore.

It's getting later and I got to get out of this house to meet my girls. I gotta look hot tonight.

Today, I went shopping. I wanted to find a hot designer outfit so I went to Neiman Marcus. I found a sweet Juicy Couture outfit and a pair of Gucci loafers. Everything was fitting to a tee. I grabbed my Gucci handbag and was out the door.

I got to Fishbone's and parked across the street from the restaurant. I walked through the door and asked the greeter about a group for Amber Smith.

She smiled, "Yes Ma'am, they have been expecting you."

I followed her and as I approached, my mouth fell open. The first person I saw was Lisa. She was smiling and then, Stacy and Kim were already seated. They'd bought a cake that they'd had a picture we took together last year put on it. It was gorgeous. I had all types of gifts. We started laughing and talking.

Tonight was a great night. Joseph was behind bars and they even arrested his mother for aiding and abetting a fugitive. I know my girl Kim could finally relax and breathe.

We were ordering drinks and having a ball. We ate all kinds of stuff. I started opening my gifts and came to one that didn't have a name on it.

I turned to my friends, "Who bought this?"

They all looked at each other as if they didn't know.

Lisa yelled out "Just open it!"

I smiled and started opening it. There was a letter with my name on the envelope inside the box. As I read the letter, I started to cry.

It was from Carrington, *"Dear Amber, Happy Birthday. I wished I could be there with you tonight, but Lisa explained to me that this was girl's night out. I just want you to know that I want to be a part of your life. I have enjoyed the days and nights we have spent together. I am so glad I approached you. I have been talking to Lisa a lot about you and she explained some things I didn't quite understand. I want to grow with you Amber. I want to be there for you in good and bad times. I don't want you to ever spend a night alone that you don't want to. Men say a lot of things, and so do women, but I want you to know I'm serious about you. About us. In this box, you will find out just how serious I am. Let's take our relationship to the next level. I want to be yours exclusively and you to be mine. Love, Carrington."*

I had tears flowing from my eyes onto the tissue paper that wrapped my gift. Lisa was clicking pictures and crying all at the same time. I opened up one box and it was a set of keys. A key chain attached said, the keys to my home. I opened up another box and it was a diamond pendant shaped like a key. He had another note in their saying, "the key to my heart."

I cried so hard. As we all dried our eyes, I saw their eyes go toward the door and in walked Carrington with a bouquet of roses. He had on a suit and looked wonderful.

He looked in my eyes, "I'm not staying. I just wanted you to have these." He gave me the roses. He then showed me the chain around his neck which held a diamond pendant shaped like a lock.

He whispered in my ear, "I'll be waiting for you at my house to unlock this lock."

He kissed me and walked out the restaurant. My girls started screaming. Now that's what I'm talking about. Lisa and

Stacy went to the restroom while Kim and I talked about the good men God blessed us with.

Lisa and Stacy returned from the restroom with their smiles completely gone. Stacy seemed to be pissed and Lisa was in shock. Kim and I looked at each other.

I asked, "What's Wrong?"

Stacy looked at me, "We just went to the bar to get another drink and Lisa recognized this woman from some club she goes to."

I looked at Lisa and back at Stacy, "Yeah, but guess who she with?"

I was puzzled, "Who?"

Stacy said, "That muthafuckin' Ameri!"

I lost my breath, "Are you serious?"

Stacy was angry, "You know I don't forget a face!"

I got up and told Lisa let's go. We headed toward the bar. We got to the bar and watched them sitting at a table laughing and talking. He held her hand. I couldn't believe it.

"Lisa, did you see that?"

She finally snapped out of the trance she was in.

"Yeah. I can't believe Ann is Ameri's wife."

I looked at Lisa, "How you know that? He could just be dating another woman. Besides, his wife's name is Angel."

Lisa got mad, "Well, it's one way to find out. Watch this!"

She put on her model strut and had the ghetto Lisa all in her voice. It was about to get ghetto up in here! Lisa went up to the table and smiled. She spoke to Ann and seemed to be speaking with Ameri. Finally she pointed over to me and I didn't know what to do. I looked in Ameri's eyes and all the color seemed to drain from his face.

Lisa motioned for me to come over to the table. I walked over and Lisa introduced me to the woman.

"Amber this is Ann. Oh, I'm sorry Angel."

She looked at me, because she recognized my name and then looked at Ameri.

She said, "Well, well, well, nice to meet you Amber."

We all looked at Ameri. Angel smiled at her husband.

"Oh, Ameri don't get quiet now."

She stood up and hugged Lisa, "How you been. I haven't seen you in a minute."

Lisa smiled, "Yeah I know. We got to catch up."

They smiled at each other. Angel sat back down.

"Well Ameri, let's hear all those good lies you been telling Amber. It's her birthday celebration, so give her the truth for her birthday."

We were handling this situation so civilized; no one around us would be the wiser of what was really going on.

Angel looked at me, "That's a beautiful pendant Amber. I have one just like it, or do I Ameri?"

He hung his head even lower.

"Look, I'm sorry Amber. I've been lying to you all along. Angel and I aren't getting a divorce. She doesn't have cancer. She told you the truth when she talked to you over the phone."

I couldn't believe the turn this night had taken. It had gone from sugar to shit in record time. I'm just glad I know what is really going on.

Angel spoke up, "Ameri, I'm tired. I don't want to go through this anymore with you. I think you really need to move in with your brother. It's over. I'm too old for this."

She stood up again, and tongue kissed Lisa and walked over and tongue kissed me. It took me back to the night at "Heaven on Earth", when we all kissed. If it wasn't for Carrington approaching me, I probably would have slept with Angel that night. How crazy is that?

Ameri was messed up. He couldn't believe his eyes.

"What the fuck is up with you Angel!?"

She smirked, "Oh, you thought you was the only one getting your freak on?" She smacked her lips, "Please!" She looked at me and Lisa, "Ladies do you mind if I join you?"

"Not at all," we said.

We walked away from the table, but before we got too far I stopped Angel and Lisa, "Hold on."

I walked back over to Ameri. He smiled thinking I was coming back to him. I snatched the chain and pendant off my neck and put it in his drink. I turned my ass around and strutted back to my girls. We headed back to my side of the room to finish enjoying my birthday.

LISA

Small world, I would have never guessed the girl I was so intrigued by was Ameri's wife. Angel is cool people. We have a lot in common. Turned out her and Ameri have been separated off and on for years.

Since Amber's celebration, Angel has filed for divorce and put Ameri's trifling ass out for good. She said the only release she had was going to the spot, that's why she was there so much.

That guy we ended up hooking up with together is a lawyer and he got someone in his firm to handle Angel's divorce. It seems they've been getting a little closer. I'm happy for her.

The lawyer whose name is Marcus, Angel, Ron and I went out to dinner. We had a pretty good time. Since we all know each other from the spot, it makes our relationship so comfortable.

Life is going pretty good. Simone is happy having her mommy and daddy in her life on a daily basis. Only problem is Ron being able to see LaRon. He has gone to the Friend of the Court and retained a lawyer and is asking for visitation rights.

203

His lawyer advised him to get a blood test to be sure LaRon is his baby. He has been requesting it, but Erica doesn't want to comply with the request. I told Ron, Erica got something to hide.

I know she was the one who slashed my tires in front of Ms. Gladys house a couple of weeks ago. I'm gonna catch her ass. I just hope Simone is not with me when I do.

We are off for the July shut-down. Ron and I are going to Cedar Point for a few days with Simone. Kim and Alan are in the Poconos getting married. Amber and Carrington are going with us to Cedar Point. Turns out Carrington loves roller coasters.

I went over to Ms. Mary's to pick up Simone. She was happy to spend some time with Simone. It had been a while since she had to keep Simone because Ron's mother had been keeping her while we worked.

Simone spent two days with Ms. Mary and was happy about it. Ms. Mary always makes her cookies and cakes from scratch. Ms. Mary was also happy to see me. She hugged me like it was no tomorrow.

"Chil' how you been? That Ron sho have changed. He dropped Ms. Simone off over hea the otha day and told me how sorry he was for all he had done. Chil' I couldn't believe it."

"He has changed hasn't he? I told Ms. Mary I was doing really well and we were taking Simone to Cedar Point. Simone overheard us and started jumping up and down.

Ms. Mary was still talking, "Ron told me he had a new son. His mama already had told me. I saw the little boy over her house. Chil' that baby don't look nothin' like Ron. Don't look nothin' like that girl eitha'. Ya'll have a blood test?"

I looked at this wise old woman, "Ms. Mary we trying to get her to do it but she keep saying 'no'. Ron is over to his mother's house seeing the baby right now. He wanted to see LaRon before we leave for Cedar Point."

I gathered the rest of Simone's things. We both hugged Ms. Mary and were on our way to Ms. Glady's house.

I got to Ms. Glady's house and Ron's car was in the driveway. Simone and I got in the house and Simone ran straight to her baby brother.

She kissed her brother, "Hi Ron Ron."

Ron was sitting on the sofa next to LaRon in his carrier. He looked at me, "Hey Baby."

I knew something was wrong, "What's up?"

"Erica told me to keep LaRon. He's been over here with my mother for two days. She just called over here and started some more stuff. She's pissed cause she knows we were going out of town."

"How she know that?"

He looked at his mother, "Mama told her."

I didn't lose my cool, "No big thing. We'll just keep him. We can go to Cedar Point anytime. Get LaRon and let's go."

I called Amber from my cell phone to tell her the situation. She understood and we got to Ron's house in no time flat. He was pissed off, but I told him it was nothing to be mad about. We put LaRon to sleep in his room and were sitting on the sofa.

Simone was taking a nap when it hit me like a ton of bricks.

"Ron, you can get the DNA test now. Call the place."

He looked at me, "You right, Lisa."

He jumped up from the sofa and called the DNA testing center.

He hung up the phone and said, "I made the appointment for tomorrow."

We were happy as hell with the anticipation of tomorrow.

The next day I sat nervously waiting for them to come back out. LaRon and Ron were done so quickly. He paid an extra fee to get the test back quicker. In less than a week we would know the truth.

Erica had been calling Ron's phone like crazy.

Finally he answered, "What Erica?"

I could hear her yelling over the phone, "Where the fuck you at with my baby!?

He was mad, "Don't worry about it. You didn't care when you left him with my mother. I called protective services and told them you abandoned LaRon."

"I know, you a bitch Ron. They came over here and took my fucking kids. I'ma fuck you up for that shit. You knew I didn't have no lights on over here. I need some money to get my lights back on. Bring my fucking son back over here."

Ron was surprisingly calm, "Erica, you don't have no room to be making demands. You asking me for money and making demands? Nah, that's not how it goes."

I could tell she was crying. I wasn't a heartless bitch.

I told him, "Take her the money Ron."

We decided to go together.

STACY

I was happy to be off work for the July shut-down. I had packed all my stuff at my mother's house. Mike and I had been moving it a little at a time. Since we were off, we were going to get the rest of the move completed.

I've become completely domesticated. I cook just about every day and Mike loves it. I love having dinner ready for him. I had to do some grocery shopping for the house. I was planning on making Mike a surf and turf dinner.

I was buying enough food for the week. I just wanted to be in the house with my man. I wanted to have enough food so if we didn't want to go out we could stay in for a couple of days.

We had planned on a 'sex day'. A day where we could sleep, wake up, have sex, sleep, wake up and have sex some more.

I was at Kroger's walking down the aisle making sure I didn't miss a beat. I bought a lot of fruit. Mike loves bananas and watermelon. I made sure I got plenty of that.

I had gone out and bought five new pieces of lingerie for five luxurious days. I got the best looking steaks from the meat counter and lobster tails from the seafood counter. I picked up potatoes to bake and I decided I was going to make an apple pie for dessert.

As I made my way from the first aisle to the last, I was on my way to the checkout. I passed by the wines and got a couple of bottles for tonight.

As I approached the register, Mitch spoke, "Hey baby girl."

I was startled, "Hey Mitch. I keep running into you. Did you move to this area?

He smiled, "Nah! I know somebody over here."

I nodded my head, "Oh, okay."

The cashier finished ringing up my purchase and I paid. Mitch was next.

"Well, see you later."

He smiled, "Okay, Baby girl."

I was at my car putting the groceries in when Mitch came up.

"Baby girl, I need to talk to you for a minute."

I looked at him, "About what Mitch?"

"I don't want to talk about it standing in the parking lot. Can I sit in the car with you for a minute?"

I reluctantly said, "Yeah, come on."

While he put his bag in his car, which was parked next to mine, I sent a text message to Mike telling him Mitch was at Kroger's.

What I thought I Wanted

I called his phone and let him hear the conversation. Mike and I had been keeping all lines of communication open, especially after Danetta told Mike that crap.

I knew Mike was listening as I laid my phone down on my lap.

"So what do you want to talk about Mitch?"

He kept his eyes looking straight ahead at first.

"I want you back in my life. I want us to go back to the same way we were. You won't even take no money from me now."

I had stopped taking anything from Mitch a while ago.

"Mitch, you know I can't be with you anymore. I deserve to be married and happy."

He looked at me, "I told you I'm not happy with Jude. You keep saying that."

He was breaking down.

"Mitch, I think you need to get out my car."

He pulled out a small handgun, "Pull off. You not takin' me serious."

I couldn't believe I was sitting in my car with a gun barrel looking at me.

"Mitch, you trippin'! Put that gun away."

He gritted his teeth, "Look baby girl, drive off or I'll shoot you right here."

I was scared to death. I pulled out of the parking space and drove off slowly. I tried to talk to him, "Mitch, why are you doing this?"

He kept shaking the gun at me, "Because you wouldn't just keep things the way they were. You wanted a relationship! Now, I don't know if I can be without you. I didn't realize I loved you. I didn't realize it til' you left me alone!"

I was trying to talk him down. "Mitch, you got your kids, your wife and all those other young girls. You don't need me."

He was really agitated. He told me to head toward Stephenson Highway. I was scared out of my mind.

"So what are you going to do, shoot me?"

He looked over at me, "I love you Stacy. You my baby girl. I don't want to hurt you. I just wanted to spend some time with you and you just kept on turning me down."

We ended up at the Fairfield Inn on Stephenson Highway. He got me out of the car at gun point. He had already gotten a key to a room and we went in. I put my cell phone in my purse and it was still on. I was praying that Mike was listening.

"Why did you bring me to the Fairfield Inn on..."

Before I could get the street out, he cut me off.

"I want you to take your clothes off and go take a shower. Wash Mike off your body."

He came in the bathroom with me. I had sat my purse on the dresser. I kept it open, hoping Mike could hear everything. I got out the shower and dried off. Mitch started undressing with one hand, holding the gun with the other.

I didn't see a way out of here. I had to play this carefully.

"Mitch is sex all you want with me?"

He was standing there buck naked, "No, I just want to see if after we have sex, you still feel the same way."

I looked at him and tried to put the most sincere face I could put on.

"I understand. I do love Mike, but I understand. We should find out."

He came over to me and started kissing me. He never put that gun down. He was kissing all over my body and I was repulsed. I pretended to like what was going on.

"Whoa Mitch!"

He was getting into me, and finally was all in. He was licking and sucking on everything. I wanted to cry.

He was talking, "Do you miss this baby girl?"

I kept saying yes.

I started crying and he thought it was because I was so happy. Finally I saw the telephone to my right. I stretched my hands over my head and he kept licking my clit.

I was able to pick the phone up with one hand and hit him over the head. I jumped out the bed and wrapped a towel around my body. I ran for the door.

He started yelling, "Stacy, come back here!"

I kept running as fast as I could. He started shooting. I felt a sting in my back but I just kept running.

The last thing I remembered was being in the parking lot and Mike's truck pulling into the lot.

E'nise

Chapter 15

KIM

Alan and I had a wonderful time in the Poconos. We got back home to find out Stacy was in the hospital unconscious. She had been shot by Mitch and hadn't regained consciousness.

I couldn't believe what I was hearing as Lisa told me the story. I rushed to William Beaumont Hospital to see Stacy.

I walked into her room and she had so many tubes and machines connected to her keeping her alive. Her eyes were closed and I started to cry.

I hoped she could hear me. "Hey Stacy, Alan and I are married now. We had a great time in the Poconos. I got something to tell you. Guess what?"

I waited for Stacy to respond and was met with silence.

"I'm pregnant! Alan and I are having a baby. I'm not going to tell the rest of the girls until you wake up."

I leaned over the bed and kissed my friend on the forehead.

"I love you, Stacy. I hate this happened to you, but I know you're going to pull through. You got everybody praying for you."

I looked around Stacy's room. There were all kinds of flowers, cards, and stuffed animals. She is well liked and well loved.

We started back to work and the Labor Day weekend was fast approaching. I had just begun to start showing, but told Lisa and Amber it was just good loving that was making me gain weight.

We were taking turns going to the hospital everyday. Mike was even spending the night there. He was going to propose to Stacy that night this whole thing happened.

He took a leave of absence from work so he could be there as much as possible. His mind was not on work at all, but who could blame him. It was hard for all of us to be at work.

We also went by her mother's house a lot, just to help her through this. Her mother was a basket case. She kept shaking her head saying she couldn't believe Mitch shot her daughter.

Things were going good with Alan and me. Malcolm had adjusted from shooting his father and we were all moving on with life.

We had to go to court and testify against Joseph. My son testified like a man. He was wonderful on the witness stand. Joseph was sentenced to life in prison without the possibility of parole. I was so happy and thankful we would know where Joseph is for the rest of his life.

Alan sold his condo and moved in with Malcolm and me. He opened up his own gym and has been doing personal training for some very influential people around metropolitan Detroit.

Life is going great for us as we await our new bundle of joy. I just wish my friend Stacy was awake to hear and see all that was happening around her.

LISA

Labor Day weekend was approaching us and Stacy is still in the hospital. I just left the hospital and the doctor says she is doing okay. She's stable. He can't really tell us when she'll regain consciousness.

We all keep going everyday, hoping for the best. Ron finally got the DNA test back and as everyone suspected, LaRon isn't his child.

Turns out, LaRon is Erica's ex-boyfriend's baby. He's in jail and she doesn't have any means to take care of LaRon or any of her kids.

213

I hate the results turned out the way they did, because Ron loves LaRon. I admit that I've even grown to love LaRon, and Simone loves her baby brother. He has become part of all our lives.

For the last couple of months, LaRon has been with us or Ms. Gladys. Erica hasn't had time to take care of her baby. Last I heard, she was on crack and been selling her body to get what she needs. They say you can see her on any given day up on Woodward.

Her other two kids are in the custody of her mother. Ron went over to talk to Erica's mother and she told him she couldn't take care of a newborn baby. She told him she was just trying to make it with the other two kids.

Ron and I have set up a court date and retained a lawyer to seek full custody of LaRon. LaRon's biological father is in jail and he has no other living family.

Erica called us from jail asking us to keep LaRon and she would do whatever she needs to do so we could take custody of him. It's sad to see a young girl messing her whole life up for drugs. I felt bad for her.

I'm on my way to the Wayne County jail because Erica is asking to see me. I don't know what the outcome of this is going to be. Last time I saw her, I broke her nose.

I didn't take anything with me but my identification. I didn't want to go through medal detectors and have stuff ringing off or have to walk back to my car to take anything back.

As I walked into the room, I was shocked to see Erica. She had changed since our last encounter. She was frail and her skin had a darkened, ashy look to it. She looked bad.

She didn't really lift her head, but looked up with her eyes, "Hey Lisa."

I almost couldn't get the words out, "Hi Erica, How are you?" as I took a seat.

She shook her head, "It's rough. I need to get out of here."

Looking at her made me realize just how strong this drug called crack is.

She looked at me again, "How's LaRon?"

I smiled, "He is doing pretty good. I took him to the doctor the other day and he has a clean bill of health."

Her chapped lips managed to make a smile, "That's good, cause' I did smoke and drink while I was pregnant."

She was real fidgety in her chair, "Well, I wanted to tell you thanks for taking care of LaRon."

I was shocked, I thought she would be cussing and fussing or even trying to fight.

"I have grown to love LaRon and only want what's best for him. He's a beautiful little boy."

She smiled again, "Yeah he is adorable, ain't he?"

We both nodded yes to each other. She got serious again.

"Look, I know I can't take care of him and I can't give him what ya'll can, so that's why I'm givin' him up to ya'll. I don't want to drag him down with me."

She let out a tear and hurried up and wiped it away. I was ready to cry myself.

"I appreciate you cooperating with us."

"This ain't about me and you or Ron, it's about LaRon."

I looked at her, "Yeah, you right."

She sat back in her chair, "So how soon can you have some papers for me to sign?"

I told her I had the documents already put together and they were in my car. She told me to go get them.

I ran to the car as quick as I could and returned to Erica. She signed the papers and we had someone who was there visiting another person witness the signatures. It was done and Ron would be so happy.

She looked at me, "You know I didn't mean for my life to turn out like this. My mother used to run the streets when I was little, so me and my brother's raised ourselves.

I found out I could make some money with this body when I was thirteen. I been tricking ever since. Ron treated me good. I felt special wit him, that's why I didn't want to let him go. I knew it wouldn't work, cause' I don't have nothin' to offer but what's between these legs. Crack helped me out cause' it eased the pain of everything. Don't get me wrong, my mama took my kids in and she done cleaned up as she got older, but my childhood wasn't no joke. Me and my older brother's use to get money from his friends cause' I slept wit em'. That's how we ate. I don't want to see none of my kids go through that."

I had to fight back my tears.

She sat up and looked at me in my eyes, "You know why I'm a good mom?"

I pondered her question and shook my head no.

She said, "Cause' I knew when it was time to let them go to someone who would take good care of them."

She sat back and smiled.

I looked at Erica and felt so sorry for her, "Erica, I want to see you get yourself together. How long are you in here for?"

She looked at me, "Hopefully long enough to get this crack out my system."

I looked at her, "Well when you get out, call me. I want to help you. I got a lot of friends that work with programs that may be beneficial to you."

She smiled, "Now, I'm going to take you up on your offer. Don't worry, I won't be one of those ones you help get it together and they come back for the child. I want LaRon's life to be better than mine. I just want him to know I love him."

I smiled and shed a tear.

"He's going to know more than that, he will know you. You got my word on that!"

We shared a smile together, "Thanks Lisa."

"Thank you Erica."

I left the Wayne County Jail feeling pretty good. The Labor Day weekend was starting tomorrow and I had a big surprise for Ron and Simone. LaRon is staying with us.

AMBER

Carrington is a wonderful man and we are spending a lot of time together. It's funny, I knew I had a good man in Carrington, but didn't see it until my birthday. God sure has a way of showing you things.

Nobody knew, but secretly I had been praying for a sign to show me what I should do. I never knew it would take place on my birthday.

Just as I was sitting on the sofa with a glass of Merlot and thinking about how my life has truly taken a 360 degree turn, my cell phone rang. Looking at the caller ID, I didn't recognize the number.

"Hello."

"Hey Amber, how you doing?" the familiar voice said.

I couldn't believe my ears, it was Ameri.

"What do you want Ameri?"

He paused, "I just want to talk to you about everything."

I smirked, "What, about how you had been lying since day one? Or how you lied on your wife? Or how you were just going to keep this thing going forever? Which part do you want to talk about?"

He paused again, "I deserve that. Amber, it wasn't like that. Angel was lying to you. We were getting a divorce, but I didn't proceed with it because of my kids."

I laughed to myself. It's funny how you will believe a man's bullshit when you love him, but once your eyes and mind are open you see and hear everything so clearly. You have no problem deciphering the bullshit from the truth.

"Look Ameri, it's clear you still feel the need to lie and I don't want to hear your excuses anymore. I have moved on with my life and I suggest you do the same. Angel is a nice person and she deserves better than you, I'm glad she woke up too."

He got pissed, "You don't know Angel. She's just trying to destroy me, destroy us. Why don't you let me come over and we can talk about this. It's over between Angel and me. I want to be with you."

I laughed so hard and paused long enough to tell him off.

"Ameri, you tried to have your cake and eat it too. Now you've lost both of us. You should have been a stand up man and made a decision, now the decision has been made for you. I've moved on and my girl Angel has moved on too."

With vice in his voice, Ameri said, "Oh, so she your girl now?"

I smiled, "Yes, she is. We don't have anything else to talk about so I have to let you go…permanently. Don't bother to call back or try and stop by. I have a good man in my life now. He is everything you are not."

"A new man, I bet he don't fulfill your needs like me."

I thought back to all the nights of passion Carrington and I shared, "Baby, he fulfills my needs and me!"

With that statement, I hung up the phone.

It was Labor Day weekend and Carrington was planning a romantic weekend for us. It turned out that Marcus handles a lot of legal business for him. With that said, Angel and I have become really good friends.

We are planning a ski trip in December. She has filed for her divorce from Ameri and it should be over by December of this year.

She told me Ameri was crying the blues during their first court date. Talking about how he doesn't want a divorce and how he wants to work it out. Angel said she is done with all that, and with Marcus on her side, I'm sure it's no turning back. He is so lame, calling me on the phone, begging her in court. I guess some guys never learn.

Ameri has moved in with his brother and Angel couldn't be happier. Carrington and I have been attending church together. Going to church keeps our relationship strong. I thank God for sending me the right man. Life is going pretty good.

The girls and I were going up to the hospital together to see Stacy. She still hasn't awakened yet, but we know she is going to be alright.

My phone was ringing. I thought it might be Ameri again because he keeps calling me from payphones. I checked my caller ID and it was Mike. He was sounding out of breath.

"Doctor Lyson called, she woke up. She woke up!"

I screamed. "Okay, I'm gonna call everybody. We'll meet you at the hospital!"

He was so happy, "I had just left the hospital to come home and change clothes. I'm pulling into the lot. I'll see you when you get here."

I hung up from Mike and called Lisa and Kim. We were all so excited and were on our way to the hospital.

STACY

Ever since I woke up, the doctor and nurses have been checking on me like crazy. I've been having some crazy thoughts in my head. I keep having flashes of people. I can remember some things, but not others.

This lady walked into the room with the doctor.

She rushed to my bedside, "Baby, how is my baby?"

Something was familiar about her. I looked at the Doctor.

"Do you know who this is?"

219

What I thought I Wanted

The woman looked so hurt as I shook my head slowly, 'no'.

She cried, "Baby!"

She pulled out some pictures and began to show me. They were all pictures of her and...and...me. My heart rate was going up and they ushered the woman out the room. Once the nurse got the woman out of the room, she checked my vital signs and asked me to try and relax.

I was struggling so hard to remember. I guess I was thinking so hard, I wasn't calming down. The nurse left the room and came back quickly. She put something in my I.V. It must have been something to make me relax.

As I began to relax, I started to daydream and so many images ran through my mind. I realized that the woman who called me baby was my mother. I remembered taking some of those pictures she showed me. My dreams were so vivid. It seems I went through my whole life.

Two hours had passed and I was able to get a few words out, "nurse...nurse."

The nurse appeared at my bed side. I was speaking so slow, "I...want...to...see...my...mother."

She smiled and darted out the room.

My mother returned with a smile on her face. "You remember me?"

I tried to smile, "Yes."

She was so happy, "Aww, baby. Kim, Lisa and Amber are in the waiting room. When they heard you had opened your eyes they came to the hospital. Mike is out there too. He had just left the hospital when you woke up. I looked at her, "I...want...to...see...him."

She smiled, "Okay."

She went out the room and in came Mike. He kissed my lips. "Hey baby!"

I managed a smile, "Hey."

He cried, "I love you so much."

Just then a flash came through my head. I remembered Mike's car pulling into the hotel parking lot. Mitch forcing me to sleep with him, the gun, everything that had happened to me came back like a flood.

"Mike...did...they...get...him?"

I could tell by the look on his face something was wrong.

"You don't know what happened, do you?"

I shook my head slowly.

He rubbed my forehead, "Well, we'll discuss all that in time. Let's concentrate on you getting better and getting out this hospital."

The Doctor came back into the room.

"Stacy, I need you to try and move your extremities again for me."

I was able to wiggle my fingers on both hands, but I still couldn't feel anything in my feet. The Doctor and Mike exited my room and soon after my girls came in.

Kim, Lisa and Amber were all standing there, smiling from ear to ear. Lisa told me about Ron and the new addition to their family. Amber told me about Carrington and how Ameri was left in the cold. The biggest surprise was Kim was now married and expecting a little girl. We were all happy.

They all knew I didn't have any feeling in my legs, but we vowed to get through this together.

As the days passed, I became stronger. Occupational therapy and physical therapy were working with me. I was doing my best when Mike was there to push me.

He took a leave from work just to be there with me everyday. Many days I lay in my hospital bed, looking at my feet. I was concentrating so hard on making my feet move.

One day I was doing my normal concentration alone when I wiggled my toes. Tears streamed down my face as I pushed the button for the nurse to come in.

Melissa, my regular nurse came in, as she approached my bed to ask what was wrong, I blurted out, "Watch this!"

She followed my eyes looking at my feet and she turned her attention to my feet. She watched as I was able to move my toes. I looked at her and smiled with tears running down my cheeks. She was crying too.

She left the room running to go get the doctor. Doctor Lyson came into the room walking briskly, "I hear you got something to show me!"

I smiled, "Yes!"

He and Melissa stood their in amazement and watched me wiggle my toes.

He smiled, "Okay, Stacy, now I need you to try and move your legs."

I smiled, "Okay."

I tried with such a force to move my legs that I damn near kicked the covers off the bed. I didn't know I was going to do that. First the left leg, then the right, it was a happy day for me.

I looked at Doctor Lyson, "Call Mike!"

As days went by, I was up with physical therapy walking. I was doing so well.

I had some nightmares about what had happened, but a therapist was working with me. I knew in time, those nightmares would go away.

Every time I would ask Kim, Amber, or Lisa where Mitch was, they would just say, "Girl, don't worry about him. You just worry about getting out of here."

I felt I was getting stronger and needed to know if that old ass maniac was off the streets. Mike came in my room. I was always happy to see my man.

"Hey sexy."

He smiled, "Hey baby."

I sat up in the bed, "Mike, I think it's time somebody tells me where Mitch is and put the pieces together for me. I mean, I remember him kidnapping me and raping me, but not a lot more."

He hung his head and picked up the phone. He called the therapist and told him it was time. After he hung up the phone, he told me he'll be right back. Mike returned with the therapist and some papers. The therapist nodded at him as if to say, go ahead.

Mike looked at me with so much love in his eyes, "Baby, I love you so much. I just was waiting for the right time."

He gave me a newspaper with a section highlighted. The headline read, "Barricaded gun man shoots ex-lover and kills himself."

I looked at Mike and began to read. It was about me and Mitch. After reading the story, Mike began to explain, "Mitch had been following you for a while. He couldn't take the thought of me and you being together. He decided to leave Jude and apparently they argued."

As Mike was telling me this, he pulled out another newspaper and the headline read, "Gunman murdered his wife first."

Mike continued, "Mitch killed his wife the day before he kidnapped you."

I couldn't believe what I was hearing.

Mike sounded so sad, "From what the police say, they argued and must have got into a fight. Some how Mitch shot Jude and stayed in the house with her body until the next day, that's when he came to my house waiting for you. He followed you to the store.

Surveillance cameras in the grocery store show Mitch following you. The abduction was caught on tape as well. Thank God you called me and left your cell phone on, because that's how the police and I knew where to find you. Mitch planned on killing you that day, but you escaped. He barricaded himself in the room and wrote a note to you and his kids, then ended his on life."

I was amazed at the story Mike told me and the newspaper articles were even more amazing. Mitch was going to kill me. I couldn't believe it. I asked for the note he left for me on the day he killed himself and Mike brought it to me. The note was a copy of the original the police kept.

It read, *"Baby Girl, I don't know if you gonna make it. If you do, I know you ain't gonna ever see me again. Once I finish this letter, I'm gonna make sure I'm gone. I'm sorry I never made you as happy as you made me. I love you and always will. I just couldn't leave Jude. Now I done killed her. I didn't mean it, we was arguing and struggling. She just kept coming at me. I don't know what happened, I guess I just snapped and shot her. After that I just wanted to be with you. I had been following you and Jude had hired somebody to follow me. I guess that's why she was so mad. She knew all about us. She even knew you had stopped seeing me and was making me mad cause she kept saying you didn't want me. I knew you loved me baby girl, I hate I didn't give you what you wanted. Now look at us, Jude's dead, you may be dead and I'll be dead after this. I guess you was right, money can't make you happy. I wanted the police to find us dead in the bed together, but you got away from me. Then the world would have known we was together until the end. Well, I'm glad we didn't have them babies you was pregnant with, cause they wouldn't have no mama or daddy right now. If you alive, I'll always love you baby girl and if you dead, I'll see you on the other side for eternity. Bye baby girl, Mitch."*

November 16, 2006

<u>STACY</u>

I have been in the hospital for over four months now. Through the help of the physical therapy and Dr. Lyson I'm able to walk out of William Beaumont Hospital today. It has been a long road to recovery, but I made it.

Thank God for my family and friends. As for Mitch, he was laid to rest with his wife that weekend following the shooting.

The media and a lot of people from the plant attended the funeral. His daughters' attended and found out the temporary girl he had been messing around with just had a baby by him. I heard she named him Mitchell Adams II, after his daddy and Mitch even signed the birth certificate.

As for Mike and I, we got engaged while I was in the hospital and are planning to go with Lisa and Ron to Hedonism III to tie the knot. I'm looking forward to becoming Mrs. Michael McKinnly. With all I've been through, no hyphenated last name for me. I'm dropping Smith and taking on the last name of the best man I ever had. Life sure has changed for me and my girls. We've all got good people in our lives now and are moving on. Some of the things we use to want and ways about ourselves we use to have are gone. Now we know what's important in life and what's not. As the old saying goes, what you think you want may not be what you need. Amen to that.

THE END

Please enjoy an excerpt of the next E'nise release:

A Safe Haven

By

E'nise

Foreword

May 27, 2008

Sitting in this small room for the last forty-eight hours has given me a chance to think and reflect on things. It's so cold and lonely here. The center-block walls, a drab shade of grey, with words others have left etched into the walls. The glimmer of light from the small window above only lets me know when day changes to night and night changes to day.

I haven't eaten since I've been here. Sure, I've been given food, but my appetite is lost. All I seem to do is sit here, with my knees drawn to my chest and think. Rocking back and forth wondering how did I get here? How did I get into this mess? I've tried the door and it's locked. I've yelled and screamed, with no response.

Just as my mind drifted back to my childhood, the doors open and I am led down a long hallway to an office, and made to be seated in a leather high back chair. As the two men leave the room, I sit there and look around. Noticing all the plaques and pictures, I begin to wonder how my Mom is doing.

Finally the door opened and a man walked in quickly, taking the seat on the other side of the mahogany desk. He reviewed a manila folder in front of him. He was going over the contents of the folder, "Umm…Emm….Hhumm."

Finally he closes the folder, and looks at me over the top of his glasses, "Well, you've led a very interesting life. How are you feeling?"

I was confused, "I guess I feel fine. I don't understand why I'm here."

He looked quite puzzled, "What is the last thing you remember?"

227

He was making me angry, "I remember waking up in this hell hole, and no one will tell me anything!"

He opened the folder again, and quickly closed it. "You don't remember being brought here?"

I was getting pissed off, "No! The last thing I remember was being in my apartment flipping through an old photo album and falling asleep. The next thing I know, I wake up in this place. I'm sure my boyfriend is concerned and will be wondering what happened to me. I need to at least get to a phone and call him and my Mother."

The man looked at me, "What about you're Father? Do you need to call him as well?"

I couldn't understand why he was asking about my Father, he hasn't been in my life for years. "I don't know where my Father is. I haven't seen him since I was a little girl."

He pulled out a pen and began to write. As he was writing, he seemed to choose his words carefully, "Well, you will be able to contact your boyfriend and mother very soon, but first we need to talk about a few things."

He folded his hands on the desk, "I'm Doctor Fargus and I will be taking care of you for a while. Your mother and boyfriend know where you are. It is very odd you don't remember the events leading up to you being placed here, but you will as time goes on. It is my job to help you through this. To help you understand what happened and why you are here. Now, let's get you back to your room and I will work on a plan of action for you."

I didn't understand what the hell he was talking about.

"Look, Dr. Fargus, I don't know what the hell is going on, but I think there has been some kind of mistake. Something is terribly wrong here. I have a career, a social life, and have never had any problems...not even a traffic ticket. Now, I want some answers and stop beating around the damn bush!"

The two men who brought me down here opened the door; the Doctor nodded and told them everything was okay.

The Doctor sat back in his chair and took a deep sigh, "Well, maybe I should give you some insight as to what is going on."

He picks up his phone and asked that the secretary bring in coffee for both of us. After she brought the coffee in and closed the door behind her, we both took a sip.

He placed the coffee cup on his desk, and looked at me with such empathy, "I hope your ready, because I am sure you won't believe a lot of what I'm about to tell you. I think the first thing you should know is, you have been charged with 1st Degree Murder..."

Order Form

To place mail orders, please send money orders payable to Second Time Media & Communications LLC to:

Second Time Media & Communications
P.O. Box 401367
Redford, MI 48240

14.95 + tax (MI sales tax 6%) = $15.85

Turnaround time is 3-4 days.

Number of Books _____ x $14.95 _____
Tax _____
Subtotal: _____
Shipping & Handling $2.85 _____

Total: _____

Shipping Information

Name:_____
Address:_____
City:_____ **State:**_____ **Zip:**_____
Contact Number (optional):_____
Email :_____

Your support is much appreciated!

Humbly yours,
E'nise

Printed in the United States
145122LV00001B/1/P